About the Author

Kari Utoslahti has worked for decades as a journalist in Oulu, Finland. First in a newspaper called *Kaleva* and after that in a local paper *Forum24*. He took his bachelor degree at Oulu University in 1994. Now his pen flies in the world of fiction. At present he lives in Vantaa with his spouse Tiina. He is also a grandpa to three grandchildren.

Papparazzi Strikes

Kari Utoslahti

Papparazzi Strikes

Olympia Publishers
London

www.olympiapublishers.com
OLYMPIA PAPERBACK EDITION

Copyright © Kari Utoslahti 2021

The right of Kari Utoslahti to be identified as author of
this work has been asserted in accordance with sections 77 and 78
of the Copyright, Designs and Patents Act 1988.

All Rights Reserved

No reproduction, copy or transmission of this publication
may be made without written permission.
No paragraph of this publication may be reproduced,
copied or transmitted save with the written permission of the
publisher, or in accordance with the provisions
of the Copyright Act 1956 (as amended).

Any person who commits any unauthorised act in relation to
this publication may be liable to criminal
prosecution and civil claims for damage.

A CIP catalogue record for this title is
available from the British Library.

ISBN: 978-1-78830-879-3

This is a work of fiction.
Names, characters, places and incidents originate from the writer's
imagination. Any resemblance to actual persons, living or dead, is
purely coincidental.

First Published in 2021

Olympia Publishers
Tallis House
2 Tallis Street
London
EC4Y 0AB

Printed in Great Britain

Dedication

To my wife Tiina

HERE COMES PAPPARAZZI!

Papparazzi is where the celebrities are! He was a paparazzo and a grandpa in same package. He had blond curly hair, Pavarotti's twinkle in his eyes and a sailor-style scarf around his neck. Our hero was always in the middle of action. He made news front pages and headline posters.

Papparazzi had moved from Oulu to Helsinki around five years ago. He had traded his former career as a photojournalist in *Ilmari* newspaper for entrepreneurship. He made the change after a divorce. Ex-spouse Raisa had stayed up north. They didn't have much to do with each other. He knew that brunette had a toy boy as a live-in partner. The divorcees had a grown-up daughter Julia living in Tammisto, Vantaa with her family. Julia was an accountant and her husband an estate investor. They had two children under school age called Nella and Eeli.

The most important sidekick to him was called Machine. The man from Käpylä was about ten years younger than Papparazzi and knew the city like the palm of his hand. Machine had a solid background in athletics. He had a cabinet full of prizes from long runs. The bachelor had an extensive collection of movies and TV series on DVD. They were constantly staring at them together.

For Papparazzi bullseye shots were more than his meal ticket. They were art. A couple of years back the chance opened to buy a full of light gallery space in downtown

Runeberginkatu. He had grabbed the chance without hesitation. At the beginning he had managed his gallery on his own, but after a while he had made a transfer into just being the owner of the business. Instead, as the front representative towards all clients and co-operation partners, he had hired Mandi to become his first recruit and later co-owner. The girl with wild curly hair and freckled face was committed to her job with passion. All the practicalities were arranged fluently. She spread around an atmosphere of relaxation and good spirit. In the gallery they had had exhibitions from both Finnish and international paparazzi. Some of the Papparazzi's shots had decorated the walls of the gallery. Paparazzo Jimi Körkkö from *The Week* magazine had also had his photo exhibition in there. American Ron Cale's exhibition had been the most attractive of them all. It had shown photos of Jackie Kennedy, Andy Warhol, Muhammad Ali, Frank Sinatra etc.

Something more glamorous was just around the corner.

BANKSY IN HELSINKI

"Hi! This is Banksy calling. I will be in Helsinki this week and I am reaching out to you offering co-operation. Starting this Monday, my works of art will be appearing all over the capital and I am asking you, Papparazzi, to photograph them. You'll get the exact locations well in advance before you will hopefully be there taking photos. The shots have to be taken quickly, mostly in a quarter of an hour."

Papparazzi read the message sent from a burner phone with a sense of confusion at the crack of dawn. Why on earth was the famous, anonymous graffiti artist approaching him? The answer could be found in the same text when he proceeded with it.

"You are the first and hopefully the only Finnish photographer I'll be in contact with in this matter. I've seen a wide selection of your photos. They really have the It Factor! Plus, there is the Galleria Papparazzi you own, the one and only in Finland, which I find intriguing. You'll have free hands to showcase your Banksy in Helsinki photo exhibition. You can also sell your shots to media and photo agencies freely — on Sunday night or soon after that. Until then I would like to work in peace."

His enthusiasm grew line by line until he finished reading. Papparazzi then sent his acknowledgement with the single word OK. Spontaneity was one of his strengths. If somebody wanted to pull his leg, there was nothing to lose. His calendar was mocking him with its emptiness. If this was real Banksy, he had nothing to lose. Banksy was delighted with his response, promising to be in touch shortly.

After breakfast Papparazzi went through his checklist on the contents of his camera bag. Everything was fine. He was always on call anyway. He was ready to go 24/7; if any of the leading tabloids or magazines wanted his expertise on any assignment, they could send him. Now Banksy was his priority. If something else was going to come up, he would reschedule it as best he could.

His smartphone peeped and he grabbed it. The first place was a wooden house in Limingantie, Kumpula. He started off. On the way he went through the basics. On the spot he was supposed to move around as quietly as possible, take photos and leave unnoticed. Papparazzi thought that Banksy played wisely by insisting him not to sell the photos before the end of the week. The rest of the world didn't need to know of his presence in Helsinki just yet. When Banksy's art became public, it was ruined in a few hours. Sometimes just painted over. People have been known to remove them from the walls, taking them and selling them for astronomical prices. This time there was no fear of that happening.

When Papparazzi arrived at the scene, he parked his silver-grey Kia on the side of Limingantie and looked around through the windshield. Few people passed by. He headed towards a large red house. He hid his camera under his coat. There was nothing special about the house at first sight. He walked around to the other side. He sighed with relief since there was no-one in sight. His hawk gaze wiped the building once more. There just wasn't anything obvious to catch his eyes. He looked around the house. Closer and further. Sometimes on all fours. Nobody and nothing! Was he had really big time now?

Just as he was about to leave frustrated, he noticed a dark spot at the foot of the flagpole. He treaded closer and his eyes widened. Photographer Rat! A witty expression on his face stretching his camera out. Papparazzi lifted also his camera and let it sing songs of joy. After taking enough shots he returned to his car.

On his way home he let out a sigh a relief. Operating on a private property was always tricky. In this case it was a risk worth taking, considering worldwide interest in Banksy's work. There are millions and billions of graffiti artists all over the world. Competition was brutal. You had to get it done quickly, mostly during the night, trying not to attract attention of the police or private property owners. That is why Banksy's rising to be the top dog had made him earn Papparazzi's ultimate respect. His way up must have been a rocky one. He was one of the most prominent artists of the day. In the mind of this curly blonde he was the voice that screamed and sung in the streets, gateways and bus stops. Although his and Banksy's values did not entirely meet, Banksy's creations always caught his attention. He had tremendous ability to make a statement in a small place.

Papparazzi spent the whole evening going through his shots in his study/bedroom. His favourite was a close-up shot of the rat. This was showcase material! At the same time, he realized that Banksy had not requested any of the shots to be sent to him — at least for the time being. His famously big posse had obviously seen to that too, the thought flashed through Papparazzi's mind like lightning.

His anxiety grew every day that passed without any contact from Banksy. Nothing to see or hear. Finally, on Wednesday his mobile phone woke up.

"Hello! You did great on your first gig. Although you thought that you were the only one at the scene, there were several pairs of eyes watching you all the time. We don't want to make any mistakes now, when the game is on. You'll get the next spot around midnight."

And it wasn't just any place! On the rock adjacent to Hietaniemi beach Banksy had painted a picture suitable for the landscape. A little girl was reaching out to catch a runaway heart-shaped balloon on a beach. In the sand under the picture Banksy had scribbled words: "This would look good in frames." Papparazzi gave some light treatment not only with a flashlight but also with his camera flash.

A girl and a balloon theme were almost Banksy's trademark. One of his most famous works of art *Love Is In The Bin*, self-destroyed in a London auction house, was also repeating the same theme. The buyer paid over a million euros for that one. The record price for his painting presenting the British Parliament House of Commons full of chimpanzees was over 11 million euros. At the time the Brexit debate was boiling over. Papparazzi concluded that the street artist had been in Hietsu making a smokescreen. After dawn people would think it was made by a local artist. Being so small in size, it might go unnoticed revealing Banksy's presence on the spot.

On Thursday Papparazzi had a gig with a leading tabloid. The Brit was well informed about it.

"I won't be contacting you today. Are you ready to rock and roll starting tomorrow? Keep your calendar empty for this weekend!"

There was a big buzz in Market Square. An old gent in a cap and sunglasses had a small stall on the far side and was selling graffiti art pieces. The colour world of the art pieces was mostly black and white. The price was 50 euros per piece. People were passing by with slow pace. Only a few of the passers-by laid an eye on his merchandise. No-one paid attention to the fact that they were signed by Banksy.

Sighs and yawns. Eating burgers and sipping water. The clock was moving like a snail.

At last a dark-haired youngster purchased a couple of paintings. They would decorate the empty walls in his student flat. In one a monkey watched through bars with sad eyes and the other one presented fried egg, sunny side up. The egg yolk was coloured yellow, the only colour in the otherwise black and white painting. Papparazzi, who was standing on guard, took his shots of the situation.

Just before closing time a talkative stay-at-home mum grabbed herself one painting presenting a protester throwing a blue and white javelin like a stone or Molotov cocktail. Jovial mummy negotiated a good bargain with 50 per cent off the price.

Click, click!

The paintings would be worth a lot more, once they found out that Banksy was the painter.

A red and white sliding door of a warehouse in Tattarisuo featured a weeping woman crouching down and holding a bouquet of flowers tightly against her breast. Flowers and petals falling around her feet. Weeper's name was visible: Dream Shattered. Papparazzi made his camera do its job at the sunset.

After his session he stayed admiring this shattered dream. These pictures with a strong emotional charge. He appreciated being able to do it in ultimate privacy. In few days the place would be crowded with spectators.

The photo session of a skeleton hanged on a flagpole outside the entrance of a pub called Ahoy Sailor! in Punavuori was due to happen at the crack of dawn. Barflies were buzzing around the clicker distracting him. It was pushed around, cuddled and talked to. It was also given a boost. People were wondering what this strike of art was all about. Why was the photographer there? Papparazzi dodged the questions as best as he could. He warned them to stop harassing the Quiet Hanger.

Let him hang in peace — just as the artist wanted it...

Desire echoed to deaf ears, judging by the missing finger and toe bones. A hipster pulled a tibia out and pushed it into his pants collar. The noose was already removed. This case was stripped to the bones. Home, especially its warm and cuddly bed, was calling Papparazzi.

Papparazzi was setting his equipment beside Allas Sea Pool. Banksy had emphasized that he needed a long tube and pedestal. The sea spa and the adjacent Market Square enjoyed the summer heat. People were splashing, moving, enjoying themselves, eating, drinking and shopping. In addition to his scarf Papparazzi was wearing a brimmed hat, shorts and light-coloured T-shirt. The view of the pier and sea was coloured with a colourful fleet of boats. A ferry was just leaving towards Suomenlinna from its pier opposite President's Castle.

A reddish worn out fishing boat was approaching President's Castle. The vessel's deck was crowded. Papparazzi squinted his eyes to see it more clearly. Arms and legs were flapping in the wind. They had to be human-shaped balloons... Banksy was striking on the sea this time. It was time to get behind the camera and start shooting. His pace was a few shots per second. The vessel's ten-metre-long deck and cabin were bursting with human figures and mannequins. The only features you could see of the skipper were his head covered with sunglasses and a hat. All the figures had coffee bean brown skin and black hair. It was obvious that his work depicted people wearing ragged clothes fleeing across the Mediterranean, putting their lives in danger. The whole boat had a spirit of desperation, helplessness, frustration and anger. Death. A boat called *The Sea of Blood* was anchored in front of the Castle, its side facing the Market Square. Blood red life rings were thrown in the water. Some of them had hands holding on to them, some had faces half under the water. A dummy fell from the boat and sunk to the bottom of the sea. You could hear voices screaming help, scratching and knocking.

People were watching from the spa and market square the macabre sight on the sea. Papparazzi was also squeezed tight in the middle of the crowd.

"What the hell is going on up there?" puffed the bald-headed old man, squeezed on the side of Papparazzi.

Papparazzi shook his head and told him that he was there just watching seabirds. "Maybe it is some artist's performance."

What else could it be? A phony artist is trying to get tabloids to pay attention. Taxpayers' money sinking in vanity again. No ordinary people can understand these things.

People's voices rose. A toddler burst into tears on the far left. Smartphones were clicking. Media people pulled in —

just in time to see *The Sea of Blood* chased away by a police patrol boat. It couldn't be helped; the boat of art had to leave the scene to broader waters followed by the authorities. All the remaining props were collected with greed. People had estimated that these were worth a lot of money in the future.

Papparazzi was quite sure that Banksy would be revealed in the aftermath of this performance. He had a lot of shots from previous gigs and these new ones he could add to his laptop in his car. Everything could be ready in a quarter of an hour. Then just press the sell button to the bottom…

He checked the latest news from his phone. The performance was notified only briefly. The artist was still unidentified.

Banksy had sent a message. The Brit would not reveal himself voluntarily at this stage. The skipper had the ultimate trust — he wouldn't snitch or betray him. He would expect the same discretion from Papparazzi. He started off listening to his car radio with sensitive ears. The magic word Banksy was never mentioned.

Saturday slid into the evening and to the night. Wild guesses were thrown around the media. The strike was thought to be political, so the strike could have been done by some young leftist activists instead of an unknown artist. Banksy was also mentioned, but in disbelieving spirit. He usually confirmed hastily in the internet, bragging about his latest enterprise. There was no such announcement on his homepage. Despite this, some art experts were leaning towards thinking that he could be the culprit. Unknown guerrilla artist was the main suspect. The conversation was intense both in media and social media. The loudest majority wanted this kind of filth banned altogether. There were just a few people who understood it. People like Banksy released art from its usual alienators like museums and institutions.

On Sunday Papparazzi's phone clicked as a sign of message. It was time to get moving. There was a big buzz going on around a yellow Kusari construction in Kamppi. The photographer had to use his elbows to get through. In the Kusi igloo you could read the words: "This is my Helsinki."

Under the balcony of the Old Student House was hanging a sheet demanding legalisation for graffities. The front of the house was crowded with people holding their mobile phone upwards taking photos of the installation. Papparazzi joined in as well starting to shoot.

On the fence of Korkeasaari Zoo lion cage there was a text: "Entertainment for you, imprisonment for us." Papparazzi was there just in the nick of time before the personnel removed the banner made of cloth.

There was an ongoing buzz about Banksy. Was the master floating around in Helsinki? Where was he now? Police announced that they were strengthening their efforts to catch the perpetrator. "Unauthorized tampering is a criminal offence," an official announcement declared. Papparazzi felt the ground starting to get hotter under his feet since he had been in every site. Banksy stayed hidden for the time being. The photographer visited the artist's homepage frequently. No mentions of Helsinki.

The twilight of the evening and Papparazzi fought his way through a wall of people towards Havis Amanda. The statue glowed in neon colours and there was Banksy's tag drawn to her breasts. Flashes flashed and loud noises tormented ears. There were naked and half-dressed men and women swinging on the mantle stand of Manta. People were also swimming in the fountain pool surrounding the statue's feet, dressed like Adam and Eve. There seem to be no space left to be found.

"Excuse me, I am a photographer."

"So are we! Don't try to jump the queue!"

Camera in its position and index finger pressing the button. Rapid-fire! Occasionally he raised his arm, continuing shooting. In the evening sun the water drops gleamed like rays of gold. He had great expectations for the best shots.

Knowledge of Banksy's presence in Finland was spreading like rings of water all over the world. The street artist and his work were chased fiercely. It was also interesting who was going cash in with this.

The clock in Stockmann's front entrance was melting like the one in Salvador Dali's painting. Or it seemed like it. Papparazzi rushed to the scene elbows first. Soon his camera flashed near the rotating clock. The name of Dali's painting was *Permanent Memory*. This was a great choice for Banksy's showstopper. He would set his mark on the art life in Helsinki and Finland. People started to talk about the times before and after Banksy.

Banksy thanked Papparazzi for his co-operation and gave him permission to start selling his shots. He had left Finland with his posse. Papparazzi took a peek in Banksy's homepage; they confirmed he had taken over Helsinki. They had also published their own photos from the artwork on their own website.

Papparazzi withdrew himself into his car to make a selection of the best shots of the day and changed then his role from photographer to a salesman. The whole set of shots from the whole week was now complete. Tabloids were purchasing shots with record prices. Some of them were published in the internet first in order to enhance sales on Monday issues.

Next week they purchased more pictures without a glance on the price tag. Daily newspapers and entertainment magazines, TV channels and photo agencies followed. Especially the major photo agencies' readiness to pay whatever made Papparazzi hyperventilate. The reason for the hunger of having the photos was because most of Banksy's artwork was not seen in its original form. Artworks in Tattarisuo, Hietaniemi and Kamppi were messed with tags and graffiti. Confiscated cloth banners, bones and life rings were waiting for the right moment. The dummy from *The Sea of Blood* was salvaged from the bottom of the sea and sold out with an astronomical price. Market place paintings were left to collect more value. They hadn't been put on sale just for the time being. In Kumpula the family sold tickets for those willing to see or take photos of the rat. The area was fenced and equipped with security cameras. The clock at Stockmann was back as it was. Nobody knew what happened to Banksy's *Permanent Memory*.

The City of Helsinki condemned most steeply the handling of Havis Amanda. The loudest in the matter was Vice Mayor Nasima Razmyar. Cleaning up Banksy's handiwork would be a very expensive procedure. In the future the statue would be guarded more intensively.

Banksy pictures were published in every media available. On the covers and on internet magazines' front pages the most-used image was rainbow-coloured Havis Amanda. Those images were also Papparazzi's favourite. Several others made his heart beat faster as well. The most eligible he would be choosing for his Banksy in Helsinki art exhibition. He and Mandi decided to prolong the time of the exhibition to six months. All signs referred to unforeseen public rush. Banksy had also notified his presence on the spot "grey as the autumn weather". Shots of the Brit would cause him to have an orgasm, but first he should be able to establish his true identity. The biggest difficulty in this was the possibility that Banksy could be a name used by a group of artists.

The exhibition started off in early autumn. At the opening there were a lot of celebrities. Media representatives were also present in such a large crowd that people felt deprived of oxygen. The chatter went on endlessly. The invited guests were photographed browsing around the gallery in admiration holding glasses of wine in their hands. There were 40 pictures hanging in the exhibition. All of the Banksy artwork was there. In front of the screen in the middle of the room were attached photos of *The Sea of Blood* and in the back Havis Amanda shots.

Papparazzi's favourite pictures were ones showing the whole right side of *The Sea of Blood*. Torn off limbs, submissive, frightened faces, blood red colour... Human cry of pain penetrated through.

Star tenor singer Antti Jyrkilä was fascinated, especially by the photo of *Dream Shattered*.

This pierces through my heart, he confessed to Mandi.

Anyway, the exhibition had a flying start. People were queuing to see it on an everyday basis. At longest the queue twirled in front of Temple Square Church. International film crews visited on a regular basis. Paparazzi were stalking around the gallery where they had a lot of chances to catch good shots. Many of the worldwide known celebrities wanted to see the newest Banksy shots. For example, Quentin Tarantino, Paris Hilton, Kim Kardashian, Conan O'Brien,

Daniel Craig and Adam Lambert had joined in the star cast. British media people were keen on the possibility of getting a photo of Banksy and revealing his true identity.

Papparazzi was also stalking vigorously on Runeberginkatu. Inside his gallery he took photos of all the celebrities with consent. Usually he never did ask anyone's permission. After saying "yes" people tend to pose when having their picture taken. Recognizing Banksy seemed like mission impossible. At this moment he could see possible suspects: tall man wearing a beret, talking to a beauty standing beside him, guy with cauliflower ears wearing an Arsenal T-shirt, joyful bunch of men, a middle-aged man with nervous eyes...

A message blinked in his mobile phone. He swiped it open. Banksy congratulated the exhibition on its success. "It was a pleasure to pass by all the photographers including you, Papparazzi, and remain unidentified. I will soon catch my flight in Helsinki-Vantaa airport. I thank you again for your co-operation ending with this message. Regards, Banksy. P.S. I hope you will be well off after selling your exhibition photos."

That's it then, Papparazzi sighed and sent a grateful reply message on its way.

Banksy's last message to him was interesting. The view of the future was bright. Pictures were auctioned on the basis of the offers. Some already talked about six-figure sums.

He would never have to worry making ends meet again.

ARCHIE ROCKS

Pop star stallion Archie, also known as Ara, pushed a woman's panties on Papparazzi's face. Pink briefs made him gulp.

"How is the smell?"

"Something other than mint and roses. I would say more like anchovies and herrings."

The macho singer burst into laughter.

"It's the real thing then! Never been washed since I got them."

The star took his turn in smelling them and Papparazzi grabbed his camera.

For decades Ara's fans had shown their admiration by throwing their briefs on stage. He was granted a title of the ultimate king of briefs thrown on stage. There were thousands of them and still counting.

At the moment they were in his one-bedroom flat in Helsinki. He had promised to exhibit his collection to *The Week* magazine. Isto Luodikko was the reporter of the story. They had wanted to call all out having Papparazzi on board. In addition, there was hairdresser/make-up artist Lilli Suutarinen. This kind of gig was more than welcome for the photographer. They were an invigorating change to having to hide in the bushes and elbowing other photographers in front of hotels and restaurants.

He had been co-operating with Archie for years. The

player knew that there was no bad publicity.

Lilli had tamed his ungroomed hair in to a new shape. His hair protruded in every direction. A blown-out look exhibited his separation anxiety. His common-law wife had packed her bags and hit the road without a word a week ago, although they had been in a relationship over a decade. Isto had vacuumed every toss and turn of the relationship into his notebook and recorder. On the living room table were lying comfort food, pizza boxes and looped sausages. The singer munched them constantly with both hands to soothe his grief. The others were not interested in the food.

Because his wallowing in his grief did not make headlines, Archie had promised to show them his panties collection. The sizes varied from granny sized to thongs. He held the first mentioned ones in his hands: they had legs and the colour was faded pink.

"May I present the sex killing pants!"

After that he grabbed the thongs.

"Those won't cover even the most vivid slit ever!"

"They will sink in your butt crack!"

All those Asian sewers must have had a field day sewing them in to one piece.

The owners of H&M have been laughing loudest on their walk to the bank. The less fabric they use the more expensive are the briefs.

Some of the panties were equipped with erotic messages. He gave a couple of examples: "I am a big lady. Can I be chubby and big for you tonight?" and "Can you take me doggy style, Oh You Great Khan!"

The yokel disco king revealed that he had given a positive response to these sirens.

Musicians are famous for getting laid more often than comedians.

On his gigs he had used post-it method to hit on chicks.

"I pick the snazziest lady from the audience and send one of the gaffers to give her a note with an invitation to my room for an after-party.

"The post-its worked like magic. I must admit that I have an advantaged position as a singer. Not getting laid land is not my home address."

So those little garments might have some bits of Little Archie in them; Lilli shot off and suggested that the singing stallion should put some of his treasures on sale. Japanese men were known from their underwear fetishism.

"Go online, get the money on your account, slip the panties into a Minigrip bag and march to the post office — easiest deal ever."

Ara was not thrilled with the proposal. He was thinking totally different use for his collection: pantyhose museum. In the museum they would exhibit panties from different decades and their evolution through times. The plan got a thumbs up from everyone.

Archie electrified the ambiance with a confession, that a group of businessmen had proposed to purchase the whole collection with a suitable price of their own. With a few tens of thousands. Isto said that he should not sell them in any circumstances. Panties were part of National Inheritance like ski jumping legend Matti Nykänen's championship medals. A reporter reminded them how Finland's Sports Museum and *Smirk* magazine had ended up saving Matti's medals with a national fundraising. Several businessmen made a claim for purchasing medals before the fundraising; Court of Appeals had ended the altercation by announcing that they were Sports Museum's property.

"There is no danger of that happening in this case. I am not in need of cash, as Matti was at times. My wallet is thick, so I am not selling my collection."

If it ever changes, Isto told him to make his first offer to *The Week* magazine. "We can guarantee that a fundraising rescue mission will be coming in that case as well."

"Nice to hear."

"And all the stories exclusively to us. As well as this one."

The couple sealed the matter with a handshake.

They heard a sneeze from the bedroom. An embarrassing silence filled the living room, where the media representatives and Archie were. None of them had made the noise. There must be a fifth person in the residence!

Ara went to see what was happening, followed by Papparazzi. In the bedroom closet surrounded with jackets and shirts there was a brunette wearing only something to cover her private parts. The star grabbed her shirt and trousers under the bed and handed them to her. She was ashamed and embarrassed. The momentum was on. Papparazzi had only seconds to get the best shot ever. He buzzed with his camera around the couple like a giant hornet. Isto also speeded up and asked who the maiden was and why she was in there half-naked. Archie and the busty lady looked at each other and gesturing to each other came in to a conclusion that the artist should be the one speaking.

"Veera came to visit me last night and we had a sleepover. We overslept. When the doorbell rang and Veera discovered you were coming in, she wanted to hide herself. We didn't want to make a number out of it, since Veera is not a public figure."

"She will be soon. We will sell our next issue with these photos. I can see the cover in front of my eyes already: Archie's secret lover came out of the closet!"

"I can understand that you are just doing your job. Without a doubt this is a juicy situation. You have a permission for publication, if and when Veera's — non-public figure's — face won't be seen in those photos."

"We can meet halfway in that, but that is furthest we will go."

The brunette nodded gratefully to Isto. She was now fully dressed and was on her way out.

"It was a stunning wake-up call. Last night was even more stunning," she cooed.

Was it really a surprise or was it staged just to keep up Archie's reputation as a player? Papparazzi was leaning towards the latter.

After the door slammed Ara was smiling like a Cheshire cat. He asked what the difference was between a random person and a celeb. When there was no answer, he let his audience out of their misery.

"Real Man is famous for having always a different woman sharing his morning shower."

After a coffee break Lilli took the joker under her wings. In a jiffy he was transformed into an elaborate gentleman. His hair was coiffed neatly and the smell of his aftershave hovered far. His grooming was in the context of the next step of their agreement with Archie, which was a sequel to be published in a fortnight's time, where he was on the search for a new bride in bars and restaurants. Everybody agreed that a beer garden tour was on the same day.

By midday the star singer attacked the streets of Helsinki on a prey followed by Isto and Papparazzi. Lilli had done her bit and headed to lunch. In Bar Con Flemari Archie made jokes to a few women, but he didn't score. Women had nothing against having their picture taken. In a sauna restaurant Löyly the charmer tried to speak to women like an angel, but the women elbowed him. They also hit restaurant Screw, of course. There was nobody looking for a date, although he was speaking like Shakespeare. Papparazzi took an indecent vertical photo of flamboyant Ara in front of Screw. Cover headline was composed right there and then: Ara had a Screw again! Also, the beer garden of Roskapankki in Kallio proved as disappointing as the others. Probably their timing was off, because of early hours of the afternoon.

In the evening Archie would ride in his car to the centre to hit it off with the opposite sex. By then lock your wives and daughters inside and throw out the key!

ICE HOCKEY LEGEND FROLICS IN KARAOKE

Papparazzi had just fallen asleep early on Sunday morning when his phone rang. These calls couldn't be missed, not with his track record. A female from Ace of Spades hinted to him that ice hockey legend Jani Pirinen had entered the premises heavily drunk. The staff had been forced to calm him, the bearded hero who retired a few years ago.

Papparazzi jumped out of his bed. Clothes on, camera bag on the shoulder and off to the road. In a jiffy he arrived at Snellmanninkatu. A phone call to the hinting lady revealed to him that the situation in the restaurant was ready to explode.

"Jani has been boozing like a sponge. Now he barges to the stage and grabs the mike off a woman whose turn is to sing. Nobody can make out what he is singing. After his splutter Jani guttered towards his table with such grand gestures that beer glasses, glasses and bottles went down. The staff gave him a final warning. He should mind his manners from now on. He seems not to get the message, since he is talking back to the staff members. I am sitting right next to that drunken bastard."

OK! I get my camera ready for action.

After a quarter of an hour the bouncer ousted the hooligan who was wearing T-shirt, summer pants and a pair of sandals in the glow of flashlight.

"What the fuck! Why are you shooting here? Drop that

gadget!"

Papparazzi said that he was taking photos of a celeb in a public place. A couple of small photos would be published in a revue nobody is reading or at least says they read. You would need a magnifying glass if you wanted to recognize the raging madman.

"How on earth did you find your way here at this hour? Was it the bouncer who alerted you?"

The bouncer shook his head.

"Liar!"

The pair started wrestling. The ice hockey player took a chokehold of the bouncer, who thwarted him with a pepper spray. Jani yelped with pain and took one step backwards.

"Now beat it! And don't come back!"

The star slogged away and stopped to puff up heavily.

The bouncer took his turn in asking who tipped him off, the loudmouth. A little white lie was a better option than the truth.

"Several eyewitnesses contacted me. At this era of smart devices people are getting in touch with me around the clock."

"You must be aware that we want as little bad publicity as Jani does. Please, do forget that this never happened."

"This is not my decision to make."

"In any case I don't want my face shown in those shots."

That promise Papparazzi was able to give him.

Jani wasn't ready to call it a night; he returned with his puffed eyes in the front door of the karaoke restaurant and tried to force himself in. The bouncer asked him strictly to hit the road. After an altercation he withdrew himself further away to pull himself together. He was joined by an unknown cyclist, who tried to talk some sense into the head of the lager lout.

There were several other curious pedestrians out and about. Photos were taken. There were rumours going around the police were coming. The drunkard had enough time to do a vanishing trick in a passing taxi. Papparazzi hopped to his car and followed the yellow cab. The hands of the ice hockey giant were flailing in the back seat. Turns to and fro. Honking. Close calls. They obviously wanted Papparazzi out of their tracks.

Finally, he voluntarily let the cab go on its way. The predation of photos was good enough already.

THE IMPERIAL SPLASHERS

A hot tip from the public had got Papparazzi on the move. The Imperial Auctioneer/Entrepreneur couple Sami and Heta Aittamäki had been spotted from Sun Beach. According to the tipster they were collecting sellable items from the capital and were having a well-earned siesta. He had also made sure that their Mercedes Sprinter was on the car park.

Papparazzi settled on the walkway that separated the beach and the nearest residential houses. He pointed his long tube towards the TV heroes. He shot pictures steadily.

The couple enjoyed their packed lunch and refreshments sitting on their towels. Their hair was damp, so they had been swimming. The coastline was only a few metres away. They had sat with their backs turned on the photographer. The positive thing was that they didn't turn their heads looking backwards. The risk of being spotted taking photos in secret was minimal. It was difficult to get facial shots. He managed to shoot some very good profile pictures. He was hoping they took another dip in the water.

Although there was a crowd of sun worshippers, they let the Emperor and the Empress coo in peace. Nobody was asking for their autographs or to have their photos taken together. Only a couple of seagulls were hovering around them hoping to snatch some treats. Heta shooed them away.

Lounging. Clock ticking. Sweat secretion.

At last Sami twisted himself up and helped Heta also to get up. Their steps led them towards the waves. Papparazzi's face became alerted. Once they were properly settled in Poseidon's empire, he continued shooting them.

The dip in the heat was obviously invigorating them. Sami pressed his nose and dived. He also took some breaststrokes. Heta splashed water on her hubby. There was also a counterstrike. After playing in the water Sami snatched Heta in his arms and carried her to the beach sand. Cover picture material! Papparazzi rejoiced.

Then it happened. Parties exchanged glances.

"Are you a paparazzo?" Sami cried out.

"No, Papparazzi!"

The white-haired man started to grab his stuff before making a quick exit from the spot. The entrepreneur couple wanted to stop him fleeing and get to talk with Peeping Tom.

"Is there any possibility for a discussion about this hit? We were busted in Crete in similar circumstances, and it wasn't pleasant to see our photos published. On the contrary we were really upset."

"We ought to talk!" Heta accompanied.

Taking a hike would be the wisest thing to do. That was not an option anymore since he felt somebody tapping on his shoulder. There was a lifeguard in a yellow shirt standing behind him.

"What are you doing here?" the youngster asked.

"Doing the right thing. There are no laws prohibiting shooting on a public beach."

"Maybe it is, but it is not too much to ask that you grant their wish. I will stand by you until they are here."

The imperial couple, the press photographer and the lifeguard caught the full attention of the beach crowd. Or at least it felt like that. It was relieving that the couple was in good spirits when they approached Papparazzi and the yellow-shirted youngster. They told the guard that his help was not needed anymore.

"We all three are consenting adults, so we can deal with this like civilized people. Can't we, Papparazzi?"

He nodded approvingly.

"Heta and me are going to the changing facilities to get dressed. After that we can pop into the beach café and talk it over," Sami suggested, and all seconded that.

The guard turned on his heels and continued his rounds on the beach.

After having hot beverages in their cups Sami and Heta confessed that they knew exactly who they were dealing with.

"You are a prestigious photographer. You have your own gallery and all. You are more of a celebrity than we have ever been."

"That's nonsense! Most guys on the street have no knowledge of my existence. You, on the other hand, are the most beloved couple in people's minds. Wherever you go, you get keen attention…"

"And envious as well!"

Sami held a lecture what their fame had brought into their life. Envy was triumphant over heat in Finland.

"When entertaining friends and acquaintances we won't be discussing shop anymore."

They tried to avoid bars as well. In Fuengirola, Spain — the southernmost suburb of our country — Sami had unwillingly been mixed in a barfight. He was never charged for it.

"That altercation thought us a lesson, that if there is only one person behaving inappropriately, the consequences can be unpredictable. A person with any sense should beat it in a jiffy."

The imperial couple liked Fuengirola a lot. After retiring from their firm, they could spend their winters in there lolling under a palm tree. The couple had sweet decades. Before television stardom they had struggled to make ends meet.

"We were usually working 13–14 hours a day. We hold an auction on Fridays in Hirvaskangas and during the weekends we do auctions around Finland. Long drives dumb your butt worse than any drugs dentists use for treating your teeth."

"This is the side people seldom see — or are willing to see."

Papparazzi felt compassion at what he was hearing. He was glad, since Sami and Heta told him that they trusted his tradesmanship on his shots instead of confiscating his camera in order to delete photos taken at the beach.

"You two have all my respect. People can see romance and relaxed living in the moment. What can be more important than that?"

The threesome got acquainted in the contents of the Mercedes Sprinter. No photos allowed. Loads of glass objects, paintings, cutlery, statues. Items bought from rockstar Virve "Vicky" Rosti, living in Vantaa, were gone through one by one. They intended to auction everything on the show and other things they were going to buy with a hell of a profit margin.

In the end Sami stripped a juicy revelation.

"We have a grandpa's moped in Hirvaskangas. If you ever stop by our lot, you are welcome sit on the rack. I will give you a royal ride."

The cameraman promised to put it behind his ear. There was no certainty since he rarely visited boondocks, that is, outside Ring Road III.

DUO RAMSHACKLE ON THE LOOSE

Papparazzi was paying a visit to his friend Machine. The twosome had dug themselves deep on the nook of the couch watching a Rocky movie. Machine had a lifelong dream of going to the stairs of the Art Museum of Philadelphia where Rocky pinned himself into physical prime by running up and down the stairs. On the top of the stairs there was constant gathering of tourists to perform the famous victorious bounce. Machine had a burning desire to be one of them.

"Some day I'll be able to gather enough money and execute my dream. I am going to run on those stairs wearing the same outfit as Rocky."

"Can you still get that somewhere?"

"I will sew it myself!"

"It's good to have some dreams in your back pocket."

"What dreams do you have?"

"Let's put it this way, my Jackie with wind in her hair still remains out of my reach…"

Papparazzi thought Rocky was very entertaining. For him it was rather a victory on points than a knockout. He'd seen better movies. Tarantino's, for example, which Machine, on the other hand, could not stand.

On the sofa table they had an assortment of savoury and sweet snacks. Beverages were non-alcoholic. There might be a gig waiting at any minute. Papparazzi had brought his camera gear just in case. Machine's Suzuki car was available for transportation.

The phone rang just before the ending of the movie when Rocky and his opponent were fighting covered in blood and sweat for the win. The *Evening News* had got a tip of a golden car in the centre. It was parked near Citizen's Square. Shots of the car and the celeb driving it, please! They needed not to be asked twice. They had already an adrenalin rush going through their veins. Outer garments on and on the road. Machine took his camera as well. They reached the Suzuki parked on the side of the street. Machine turned the key, but all he could hear was a rasp. He wiggled it on the lock without a sign of life. The driver cursed like a demon.

"I went to the grocery store yesterday without problems. What the hell is the matter with this now? Why is it acting up now, when the game is on!"

Papparazzi tried to reassure his cursing pal. The battery was probably the culprit. Machine couldn't remember when he had it changed last time. In any case it had been several years ago. He had skipped services on his elderly car. Machine opened the bonnet. By the look of it there didn't seem to be anything wrong with the engine.

"Did you forget to turn off the lights last time you were driving?"

Capheaded guy checked them. He had turned them off, but then he started swearing again.

"I left the internal lighting on and it drained the battery!"

Since Papparzzi's own Kia was parked in his own backyard stall in Tilkankatu and they were in a hurry, they needed neighbourly help in recharging the battery. Eki from upstairs gave them a helping hand. Machine's foot was heavy on the accelerator.

After having a turn from Mannerheimintie to Töölönlahdenkatu the Duo Ramshackle became alert. Would the golden vehicle still stay put on the scene? They got lucky behind Sanomatalo. Papparazzi jumped out with his camera and Machine stayed in the car listening his car radio. Though it was late night, the light was still good. The golden vehicle was photographed from the front, back and sides. There were no licence plates, so the owner remained a mystery. The enigmatic car was so stripped off and full of holes that it could not be driven anyway.

They deducted that this was a work of art. It drew the attention of pedestrians who were passing it. Selfies and pictures together were taken. Would the artist arrive to admire their work of art? They had no idea. Since they have arrived in the centre, the twosome decided to stay put. Hour after hour passed them sitting and contemplating. Just before they had decided to take a hike, they heard an exclamation:

"Paparazzi!"

Papparazzi grinded his window open and saw a dark-haired woman in her sixties approaching them. Large earrings dangled in the same rhythm as her steps. In a jiffy she was standing beside the wheels.

"Are you two paparazzi? I want to lose my tabloid virginity!"

"There are two p's in the middle."

"Papparazzi?"

"Exactly! How did you know we were here?"

"I was spending time in Granny Tunnel and my pals told that they had seen a photographer circling around my work. I got very good notes on your appearances and this dark blue car. Then I took a couple of advisory drinks before I left to have a peek if the media was still on surveillance in here."

"How's the buzz in the Tunnel?"

"Joyful, free and relaxed — as always. Engagement rings mysteriously missing also tonight. This granny seemed to find her pappy somewhere else than Old Commercial Alley."

Granny identified herself being sculptress Anna-Helena Hangas-Vuorio. The creation was called the *Golden Car*.

"I am examining the meaning of the car to people. For one person it represents wealth and power; the other sees it as an environmental polluter. I don't want to point fingers at anyone. Everybody can make their own interpretation on this lace-like patterned vehicle."

She gestured towards her work.

"Let's go and bake some invigorating scandal beside my little gold chip."

The daredevils stood out of their car with their shooting gear and followed the artist. Once Papparazzi was starting his work, several males and females barged around Hangas-Vuorio. They were wobbling drunk. Their clothing varied from shabby to chic.

"No photos!"

"Did you guys set us up?" Machine was astonished.

"Yes! We are tucking you in there! Then we get sellable sensation pictures!"

A maiden in her colourful garments compared paparazzi with vermin.

"Why can't you leave people be? Why are you fattening your wallets by taking trashy photos? You make people sick!"

Papparazzi told her that they were working their night

shift for one newspaper whose name he refused to mention. Talking sense was not an option judging from the mob's reaction. They grinned and did other odd gestures. The mob came to his face. He was pushed and ripped from his scarf.

"Didn't you hear, no photos!"

"The artist herself asked us to take her paparazzo virginity…"

"She honeytrapped you. To be honest we all wanted to get the chance to reveal what we think of vultures like you."

"Now you have done it. Would you mind letting off me?"

Machine started shooting the whole show. Clicks and flashes confused the attackers. Heads turned towards him. Gazes flamed with hatred.

"Let's run to the car!" Papparazzi roared.

The camera heroes dashed off, the mob on their heels. After getting inside the Suzuki Papparazzi closed the window and both locked their doors. One of them hit their bonnet, another twisted the antenna, the third one grabbed the back bumper and the fourth one tried to stand in front of the car, blocking its way.

"Speed, dammit!"

SUGAR-COATED POLITICIAN

Papparazzi was having a late lunch on the patio of restaurant Kappeli. While he was going through his creamy salmon soup, he was reading the newest issues of entertainment magazines and tabloids. He counted that they had published nine of his photos in them. One of them was a cover shot. The more important thing was to stay in touch with current affairs. Articles, ads and events columns gave him a good picture of who were the hottest names presently. They also showed where they would perform next and which clubs they preferred. He took notes of the best options.

Stars were like common people, they were social animals. They did their shopping in the same shops, the same hangouts for eating and drinking and also booked rooms from the same hotels. It made it easy to follow their tracks.

Well, well, well! At the table next to him sat sensational politician Terho Hartikainen. He was accompanied by a flashy blond young female. Her lashes were extended and nails were polished. Her dress licked her figure. Her nipples were sticking out, indicating that she didn't wear a bra. Her perfume scented heavily. The beauty started immediately shooting pictures with her mobile phone. The gentleman took also photos of his companion. She gave him exact orders what to shoot. A lot of giggling and cooing. Several kinds of starters were ordered and a sparkling beverage to flush it down.

Sugar baby and sugar daddy!

Papparazzi slowed down his spooning and slid his camera bag further away, so it wouldn't stick out to the neighbouring table. It was easier to let the situation evolve at its own pace before he could make his move. He pricked his ears. The woman listed all her shopping at trendy stores. There would be a sequel.

"Your sacks are not full yet... I happen to know somebody whose sacks are in need of emptying."

"Don't rush anything. All in good time!"

First portions were brought. The damsel was fastidious and returned one of them. The waiter was sorry because the food was not good enough and promised some other portion on the menu instead. The blond maiden went through the menu and pointed out all she wanted with her fingers. The Member of Parliament was astonished. He would have wanted to taste the returned portion.

"Remember the name of the game: you obey my every wish."

The compensatory dish was brought to the table and they ate in silence.

Papparazzi started to fiddle with his phone. There he found a lot of data about sugar babies. They were expensive escorts. The phenomenon was growing exponentially in our country. In most cases sugar dating was all about an older man paying a younger woman for company. The girl gets some cash and various gifts: garments, make-up products, trips, whatever's around. On the websites offering sugar dating selling sex was strictly prohibited. Yle had taken an investigative approach on the matter, discovering that soliciting sex was openly on the list.

Papparazzi put his phone down and started to pay more attention on goings on with the sweet couple at the next table. The lady went through her price list. Early evening shopping and entertainment cost him a few hundred euros. Additional services at his hotel suite would be discussed later.

Entrées were served in front of them. On Hartikainen's plate steamed reindeer and his companion's choice was pikeperch. The waiter popped open a bottle of red wine and gave a tasting to both of them. It seemed to be suitable.

Papparazzi ordered coffee for dessert and waited for the right moment of his impact. It was due just before he finished his after-meal coffee and the couple at the next table were on their third glass of wine. He rose from his chair and waved his mobile phone.

"Since coincidence led us sitting next to each other, I am hoping to get a few photos taken as a memento of this occasion!"

Hartikainen seemed delighted and gave his permission without hesitation. He straightened his upper body and turned on his posing smile. Papparazzi gave him an impression of concentrating his shooting to the parliamentarian only. Actually, the photos revealed the sex bomb as well. In some of them her gaze was fixed straight to the camera. Papparazzi bowed his head thanking him and withdrew himself back to his coffee. He contemplated the matter. Only one or two of the photos would appear in the next issue of the *Week*, probably in the gossip column. There should be more buzz going on. The chick announced she was going to go and powder her nose. Every customer in the clientele watched her catwalk performance. The photographer's light bulb lit up. Politicians need publicity! If nobody saw you, you didn't exist. The accomplished prowler formulated a bait that the knight of the people's power might seize. Thus, the exchange of words with him was in order. Papparazzi revealed him his true identity, who he was and for what purpose he had encountered the person sitting opposite. He couldn't have helped hearing that there was going to be some buzz later that evening. Hartikainen got his message loud and clear and revealed that he had booked a room in Hotel Kämp. Papparazzi asked when he could expect them to return to the hotel. Around midnight, he estimated. Could Papparazzi stake out Northern Esplanade to capture their arrival there? The request tickled the user of the power, envisioning megasized headlines in his mind.

"What the hell! We could surprise Joanna in big way, can't we?"

"Of course. I will manipulate the photos so she won't be recognized. We will give our readers a chance to keep wondering who your new girlfriend is."

"Sounds good!"

Having reached understanding Papparazzi paid his bill, bid farewell to Hartikainen and hit the road.

He didn't cross paths with Joanna, which suited perfectly for his dealings with the parliamentarian.

The bush photographer stalked the sugar-coated lovebirds with frustration. They had partied until the early hours. Hartikainen could have stood him up or just bluntly lied by telling his story about going to Kämp. It wouldn't be the first time that Papparazzi's leg was pulled. Anyway, he wasn't going to give in. His first shots had turned out exemplarily. The *Week* had agreed to buy them, but given him a thumbs up for the night shoot.

After losing practically all hope, it boomeranged back.

Joanna and Hartikainen returned back to the hotel a little tipsy. Papparazzi charged behind a tree and started shooting determinedly. Hartikainen was all on the board and squeezed her nearer. Even kissed her.

"Fine! Keep up the same thing!"

Joanna flinched and pulled away from the representative's grip.

"OMG! Paparazzo!"

"No, I am Papparazzi!"

"You were shooting us earlier. Why are you stalking us?"

The shooter steamed on without response. Joanna turned to watch her companion and told him to do something to stop the flashing of the flashlight.

"We don't want this kind of scandal! Do we?"

Hartikainen captured the blonde under his arm and encouraged her to be brave.

"Our destination is only a few steps away! Now just put foot in front of the other, that way we can get rid of that buzzer!"

Papparazzi let them go voluntarily. He had got what he was after.

GET THE FUCK OUT OF HERE!

Rock legend Mick Morrison and his spouse Theresa opened their Special Explosion art exhibition displaying their colourful art in Hard Rock Café. Paintings told stories of their eventful life.

"Holding a paintbrush in my hand I feel great!" Mick revealed to *Evening Paper*'s reporter Bella Sieppo.

Papparazzi circled around, viewing paintings with Mandi. They both had brought their camera gear with them. Mandi had loved photography ever since she was studying arts. She was still into it with passion. Artistic photos were her thing; aiding Papparazzi was something she did only occasionally. This time her assistance was available, if necessary.

Dressed in her knot-dyed clothes and self-made jewellery Mandi blended into the crowd well. Papparazzi was also wearing a festive outfit for the event. A brightly coloured dotted scarf was a spot-on pick for this occasion. The exhibition had not struck any chords with neither of them. The most expensive works of art were priced at thousands of euros, which made Mandi gasp with horror.

"Nobody in their right minds should pay that kind of money for these amateurish scrawls. Without the name Morrison nobody would exhibit these paintings."

After making a toast the rocker posed in front of the paintings with his spouse, until it was Mandi's and

Papparazzi's turn. When Mick heard who the client of the latter was, he flipped and asked them to leave the premises immediately.

The situation became volatile. Mick bolted to Papparazzi, pushed and threw blows at him and also yelled at him right to his face.

"Get the fuck out of here!"

Although Mandi and Papparazzi were dumbfounded, the redhead recognized that now was the time to push on. She shot photos with a smoking forefinger. Other people present followed the scuffle with a feeling of confusion and fear.

Staff members of Hard Rock Café intervened in the situation and pulled the baffled rock star aside. He asked repetitively the shooter and his associate to leave the premises. Theresa came also to plead with her spouse to calm down. Finally, Papparazzi and Mandi left the scene baffled.

Mandi checked him for injuries.

"Your face is blushing, but I don't see any contusion." Mandi said.

"OK. My choppers feel intact as well. I have been in worse situations during the course of my long career," he stated.

"Why did Mick flip out so totally? Are you acquainted somehow?"

"We have never laid eyes to each other before today. He is holding some kind of a grudge towards *Smirk*, but I doubt we really want to know what goes on in the corners of his mind. It can relate to his times as a member of Saigon Shakes. Maybe some reporter crossed his path the wrong way."

They were also contemplating if the rocker just wanted to pull a publicity stunt.

"It is a possibility worth considering. He has learned his big world lesson how to get media attention. Raise the hell!"

"This episode was not a done deal — that is something we both know for sure."

"This time you are the one selling the photos... They will be covering the whole edition of *Smirk*!"

HOLE IN ONE ON THE PLAYING FIELD OF LOVE

Tell me who you follow and I tell who you are. This sentence crystallized ways of modern man and their thinking. Aarno Ryck had accomplished a lot with his YouTube videos. He had hundreds of thousands of followers. He was followed by fans asking to be photographed together or an autograph.

Machine had told as a fact to Papparazzi that the YouTube star was spending his night sitting in the beer garden of Teerenpeli in the centre of the city. The photographer had sealed a deal with *Evening Paper* that he could catch good shots of the barfly. Ever since the star had revealed a tormenting fact about his personal life. He had broken off with his girlfriend. He had pleaded his fans to leave his ex-lover alone. Papparazzi had also checked the video.

The camera bloke had placed himself on the patio of Steam Hellsinki opposite Teerenpeli and zoomed the celeb from there. Evening time with diminishing light had made the circumstances challenging, but he was convinced that he could record Aarno having a feast. He took cover behind a fence of greenery. Hero was drinking mocktails, he had converted into a teetotaller a while ago. The shooter started clicking his camera buttons at a steady pace. Entourages started to pile up disturbing his shooting. He had to move forward nearer his target. Sparkles in your face.

Two young men in black emerged in front of Papparazzi from Teerenpeli. Aarno made his way to the scene too. He was dressed more casually. His suit was white and his shirt had flower patterns in it. They all wore sunglasses. Men in black said they were bodyguards, asked him to stop shooting and started pushing him around. They had a big world spirit in them. The scarfed hero was scared of the state of his choppers and general well-being for a second. Would there be a blackout as well? The attackers couldn't keep a straight face, they all burst out laughing. It was obvious that they were out to have a blast.

"We have been shooting Aarno's new video. Honouring the Tubecon we put a plot of secret agents together."

"Way to go!" Papparazzi introduced himself, promised to let his attackers go for the time being and continued: "I will send you an invoice from my laundry. That is for causing yellow-brown speed stripes in my boxers."

The youtuber was thrilled with meeting such a top-level photographer.

"There have been people secretly shooting me previously, but it is a great honour to be photographed by a master of his trade. A thousand thanks!"

"In that case, can I take some more pictures?"

Permission was granted.

When he had his picture quota completed, Papparazzi bid farewell to the trio shaking their hands. He skipped around the corner, but didn't leave the scene. His sixth sense urged him to stay put near the Kamppi Centre. After couple of hours Aarno strode in the open holding his mobile phone on his ear heading towards Tennispalatsi. Papparazzi followed. Under a red tram stop designed by Stefan Lindfors, the youtuber met a sporty chick whose blond hair was drawn back in a ponytail. They clutched each other. It was crystal clear that the youtuber had found a new sweetheart. The embrace seemed to take forever. Long enough anyway for enabling Papparazzi to record it. The tender moment went on in the seat of the tram stop. The quantity of frames was increasing. Although the flashlight resembled fireworks the lovebirds couldn't care less about the distraction. They only had eyes for each other. When the photographer was finished, he bowed gently and left the stage.

Once the first sensational photos were published Papparazzi found out that the other party of this secret romance was top level tennis player Sini Kemppainen. The beauty had resided abroad for years and moved back to Vantaa, Finland just recently. According to *Evening Paper*'s exclusive they were so madly in love that their feet barely touched the ground. The world shone around them as rays of sunshine.

Papparazzi folded his paper happy, maybe even feeling sorrow. How long had he lived in solitude? He was not opposing a new relationship, but he was not forcing it to happen. Would a wonderful apple blossom emerge by his side some day? Why was he contemplating this? He shook his head with scepticism. Forget these thoughts! There was no point in chasing the impossible.

GRANDPA GANG MEETS TERRY TICKLER

Famous Terry Tickler movies' main location and the home area of the main characters was situated in Kartanonkoski in Vantaa. This summer they were filming the next sequel again busting their asses off. Terry Tickler alias Sakke Koukkula and other child actors came to Shopping Mall Jumbo to meet and greet their fans after the day's shooting. Papparazzi arrived to the central square accompanying his grandchildren Nella and Eeli. Their parents had gone to Turku and left the kids with him for a sleepover — provided he didn't get a call on duty. Although his calendar had been empty today, that is Friday, as it happened he was alerted speedily to arrive in Jumbo this afternoon with reporter Janita Lind for *Evening News*. She wanted to cover a more profound story of Sakke. This event meeting fans would provide good material for illustration of the interview. He also wanted to take a few shots of Titsy Wisphead aka Minttu Friman and Vesteri's actor Jusa Aaltonen.

After having a treat in Ice Cream Parlour, grandpa went through cameras in their smartphones. During the past few months he had revealed to them the secrets of their smartphones. Now was time for their rite of passage. The buzz around the stars was so intense that it was difficult to fit in the mix. Papparazzi climbed on a bench and shot a few photos of the crowd. Janita picked actors one by one in order to interview them individually away from the crowd. They were able to include a few of the fans. Flaming red headed Sakke took the first turn in his own right. Nella and Eeli were radiantly happy meeting him. He posed briskly for a photo taken together with the siblings. Sakke posed in photos like a pro and even flashed a broad smile. He also gave autographs.

Janita started the interview and Grandpa Gang shot photos. Nella and Eeli focused on working hard. Looking from a distance it looked rather comical. The redhead's summer had been quite scheduled. In the mornings he was whisked off from Töölö to the filming site. After an on-site makeover and changing in to their costumes they started filming. They had eight-hour days of shooting. Today they had finished exceptionally early due to Meet & Greet.

"I've had really good time! Time just seems to fly!"

His photos were constantly on display on ads and supersized on outer walls of movie theatres. People greeted him on the streets more often as Terry Tickler than as himself. He had a very mature attitude towards fame.

"I haven't let it give me a big head. For my pals it is not that much of a big deal. They might sometimes ask how your shooting goes — that's all."

Isa and Aino had dressed themselves in flamboyant attire for the occasion being the chosen few who actually were allowed to follow closely Sakke's appearance in a blaze of publicity. They wanted to know what his favourite foods and drinks were. Basic stodge and soft drinks were his preferred supply. He didn't have a girlfriend.

"How about?" Girls blinked their lashes.

His answer was ambiguous; in fact he turned them down

gently. If ever he had a long-lasting courtship he would like it to advance at a slow pace. Aino and Isa demanded him to describe what he expected of his future girlfriend.

"I appreciate inner and outer beauty as well as brains."

Minttu and Jusa had their turn at sitting on the hot seat as well. Finally, a whole bunch started off circling on the hallways of Jumbo and Flamingo. Grandpa and the children spent another half an hour enjoying the fun before parting their way.

After coming home, they rushed to the computer. They all wanted to see their transcripts on the big screen. Nella and Eeli had pulled off their shots very well. Grandpa let them choose their favourite shots and printed them as mementos. The shooting trip scored ten points from both kids. They declared as a fact that life and the world seemed a lot bigger when you looked at it through a camera lens. Grandpa sent some of the photos to the editorial office. This time he preferred his own shots; in few years the situation might be different.

They packed their lunch and left to the Banner playground to have a run around. Swings and monkey bars were all in good use. The amphitheatre was the base for their picnic lunch.

They had so much fun at the playground that they stayed there until dusk, then returned back to Tilkankatu. While walking hand in hand the kids told him the most heart-warming truth.

"You are the best grandpa in the whole wide world!"

STARS HAVING A SCALDING HOT HUSTLE

A red-hot tip had mobilized Papparazzi and Machine. Actors Henry Vuorinen and Riitu Kekäläinen of *Hidden Lives* were smooching in a café. The Duo Ramshackle planned their tactics outside Kaffa Roastery. In the television show it was known as Moose. Henry's character in *Hidden Lives* was Ari Neuvonen, a wine merchant, who was as crooked as a corkscrew. Riitu played the role of Anna Pohjola, who was his employee. Anna and Ari were having a fling and according to a recent tip so were the actors in real life. Love has no age, since Henry was forty-five and Riitu in her early twenties. The site was well chosen. It was a place of memories for both of them; now they were creating some new ones.

Duo Ramshackle's strategy was nailed in seconds. Their actions were acted just as promptly. Machine went inside to grab himself a cup of coffee and found a seat near the lovebirds. He had a good visual contact and earshot of them. The first text was sent: "AAs sitting face to face holding hands. They are making eyes so intensively that I doubt they are leaving any time soon. They haven't finished their coffee yet either."

Papparazzi, stalking in Pursimiehenkatu, read the message with a smile on his face and nestled in a waiting mode. He had a good vantage point for visibility. It took nearly half an hour before the crucial message reached him. "AAs putting their coats on. Raised alert!"

Papparazzi run at the opened door and lifted his camera. The secret lovers were totally surprised.

"Blimey!"

"What now?"

It meant that the hot love story needed to be sealed with photos. Now they were coming of their own accord.

"Henry! Do something!"

The actor grabbed Papparazzi's hand and twisted it down. His forefinger stayed put on the trigger, although his view angle flipped.

"Why are you stalking and shooting us? Can we talk of this matter like consenting adults?"

Papparazzi nodded and pulled himself off from the attacker's grip. He passed on his business card.

"Oh, it is you! We have heard of you, but this is the first time we meet this way, don't we?"

Papparazzi granted the fact and shone light on the current operation in a vague manner.

"How could you tell that we weren't there just as colleagues, as friends?"

"I received confirmed facts on you to having a romance."

"This thing is still news to us as well. We realized it ourselves only couple of weeks ago. We made an agreement that when asked we will state the fact of having a love affair. The contents of our relationship we won't reveal. This time you asked and I answered."

"Thank you and congratulations! I tend to be where things take place and make a bang."

"So it seems! I have no idea what I was thinking coming

on to you like that."

Papparazzi assured him that there would be no backlash.

"It was only a scratch on my thick skin."

The lovers were relieved and moved on. Papparazzi went inside and bought Machine another cup of coffee. Machine told him that his ears were burning when he listened to the stars sweet-talking.

"You cannot separate those two even with an iron bar. They are so smitten."

Machine watched next week's episodes of *Hidden Lives* in advance and revealed the most important plot twists.

"I have no need for watching it — anymore."

"I ask you a trivia question. What naughtiness was Anna up to on these premises?"

Papparazzi gave it a thought, but failed to find the answer.

"You could do well in *Do You Want to Be a Millionaire?* quiz, as badly as Finland's Whiz of Quiz Erik Toivanen. He didn't make it through trials, when they asked them to align cup sizes of women's bras."

"Yeah, I guess. Are you going to tell me the right answer?"

"Anna didn't have sex in Moose with Ari, but with Tare Onninen. Anna's son Jarkko was conceived then and there."

"Oh, come on!"

The *Hidden Lives* theme went also on Machine's pad. He was adamant to show him an old episode where Anna and Ari were on. His legitimate business he used to cover up his dubious activities resided in Manta Inn where Anna sweated as a cleaner at that point. Mister moneybag was not happy with her cleaning job and ended up having a bucket of dirty water thrown on his face.

Those scenes are scarcely played in real life.

Romantic flame would go out on the spot.

Machine's generation had grown up with *Hidden Lives*. He was planning a *Hidden Lives* pilgrimage and encouraged Papparazzi to take part on the tour.

"We could check all the pivotal buildings and sets. Let's have a trip in the past and commemorate what kind of foolish things they have encountered over years."

Papparazzi declined politely.

"I haven't got enough fascination in *Hidden Lives* to take a tour like that."

Machine had got stuck with the idea of a dream trip like a glue. He had also given a name to it.

All the roads lead to Pihlajakatu.

CITY VERSUS BACKWOODS

The hostess of *Farmer Wants a Wife* TV show Laura Valkea sat with hearts in her eyes in Fazer Café Forum. Opposite her sat a man wearing a flannel shirt; his dark hair had a neat parting. Papparazzi had slammed the scene as soon as he had heard that blond family woman was slurping coffee with her secret lover. She was all pressed and powdered. On the scale from 1 to 10, this tip was 10+. The photographer was trying to be as invisible as one could be on a busy central square. He hid his camera under his coat. He already had some shoots in his pocket.

Laura's hands swished back and forth and she was radiating from ear to ear. The man was more cautious, mainly nodding and answering sparsely. Papparazzi was so far away that he couldn't hear their conversation.

Papparazzi contemplated the state of Laura's marital partnership, which would be finished soon. She had a couple of children and a filthy rich husband. They've had some critical phases in their marriage, but they had been able to overcome them. Laura spoke openly about her marriage; her spouse Ossi eluded publicity. No hard feelings, but she was facing a big fall on the battlefield of her partnership. Maybe this ex-wrestler Alexander Karelin-lookalike secret lover possessed some other virtues, he reasoned, and took yet another photo.

The new couple stood up and left the café. Papparazzi noticed that he was wearing coloured camo pants. Let's get some fireworks! The photographic subjects couldn't care less. Maybe they had sorted everything out and were ready to let everything out in the open.

"Paparazzo! We are not smooching here. If you have that idea, you couldn't be more wrong," Laura pointed out.

"I am Papparazzi! There is another P in between As. And that's what they all say!"

"I am sorry to take your scoop away right now, but we were just having coffee back there on a friendly basis."

Her companion verified her statement. The hostess ascertained that Papparazzi could still get his story. It turned out that Arttu from Velkua was participating in the new season of *Farmer Wants a Wife*; this was his first ever visit to Helsinki. Laura had agreed to introduce the capital's beating heart to the yokel. Arttu extended his peelsized hand and shook Papparazzi's hand. Laura gave him a hug.

"We have just started our round. Team up with us and shoot some photos while we explore the centre."

Papparazzi didn't have anything scheduled that day, so he agreed. Although his original idea had gone down the drains, this story would sell as well.

The redneck from dumbass hick town pondered the city dwellers' looks and their hectic lifestyle. The trio zigzagged through the crowd to the railway station. The hillbilly felt lost. They escaped the hustle bustle to Burger King for lunch. The yokel let Laura order his meal as well.

"You have a better knowledge of the finer details of the menu in places like this."

The hillbilly immediately pointed out Eero Järnefelt's

handsome nature painting on the wall of preserved Eliel Hall.

"My eyes rest in there."

His food tasted like industrial fluff.

"This is not meant for human consumption, is it?"

The yokel's gut started to rummage. His forehead was sweaty.

"Can't help it! I've got to shit!"

He was given detailed directions to the nearest loo. Laura revealed the reason for Arttu's visit to Helsinki. She pressed Papparazzi to keep it to himself until the sequels were shown. He promised to keep quiet.

The production company wanted to offer Arttu this experience because at this point it is clear that the man from Velkua will be a controversial character in the show and will gather a lot of viewers in front of the telly.

Arttu had told his prospective wives to accommodate a mobile home in the backyard.

At nighttime they were not allowed to enter the house since the master of the house is still a male virgin.

The thing he is ready to lose with Miss Right.

He didn't let the ladies use the toilet indoors. They had to use the outhouse.

The ladies had to get up at dawn to sweat on the farm work. Working was so hard that they had aches and pains all over their bodies the next day. Laundry, cleaning up and cooking were their daily tasks also.

The stingy and chauvinist farmer was struck out in the end.

After having their lunch, the hostess and Papparazzi kept wondering where the yokel was lingering.

"Did that slippery Sam manage to get lost although I

spelled it out to him?"

Laura didn't have Arttu's contact details. They got his mobile number from directory assistance. Nobody answered the phone. They had to turn to a security officer. They had no notion of a person lost in the sea of people. They did not want to take a look at the security footage since the yokel had been missing such a short period of time. Laura and Papparazzi searched him from underground and over ground. They had no idea where he was!

Just before Laura was about to call an emergency number, she heard a ping as a sign of a text message. It was from Arttu. As it turned out he had taken the first train to Turku. The commotion in the city made his nerves jump all over the place. He had to take a hike back to Velkua.

"I am suited best to the peace of the most wonderful countryside; the metropolis is not my cup of tea."

GOLD, PLATINUM AND DIAMOND

If Papparazzi had worn glasses, they would have steamed opaque. He focused on a small trimmed brush that had just emerged. Photos cascaded. The pussy was Iines Riekki's, former Miss Finland, model and TV personality. Although she was a celebrity in Finland, she wanted to startle and take part in *Naked Attraction* date show. They were filming it in Media City UK studio in Manchester. The plot was that a fully clothed male or female was looking for a perfect match from this sextet. This time the game opener was an Italian singing student Mauro Columbo, who was wearing tight jeans and a pink jacket. Curly hair gleamed with gel. Hostess Judith Richardson noticed that something was trying to escape from his fly. Naked bodies were revealed gradually starting from below.

Papparazzi had exclusive rights on her stunt for shooting to a national KasiTV. It was obvious that this was going to provoke a sensation. He had talked with Iines a few times before the shooting. She had revealed honestly that she wanted to make her naked appearance as memorable as Kata Kärkkäinen who had made a commotion with her *Playboy* pictures at the end of 1980s. Iines wanted to shake off her girl next door reputation as well.

Mauro voted out the first candidate. Since Iines was

qualified to move on Papparazzi was able to take snaps on her rack. He could not stop flashing. Mauro wanted to look closer at Iines standing in a yellow booth. He wanted to know if her breasts were natural. Because the girls were not allowed to talk yet, she just showed proudly thumbs up.

When there were only four girls left their faces were revealed. Mauro accompanied the hostess circling around them, commenting on what he was seeing. He told Iines that she was a dark-haired looker who probably was not British. The handsome contestant revealed that the hair colour was not crucial to him. The women had a hard time keeping a straight face listening to his arguments. Papparazzi shot like a sniper in WWII.

Iines made it to the final three. This time they were also allowed to speak.

"A pleasant sound means a lot to me," the Italian admitted.

All of them were asked to tell their favourite song. Iines told that hers was Timantit on ikuisia sung by Cheek; she also gave a sample of it.

"You're a Finn. What is it about?"

"Diamonds are forever."

"Good set."

"Marilyn Monroe also sung that diamonds are girl's best friends," the hostess said and asked curly to describe maiden Finland with honeyed words.

"Tits are made of gold, pussy is pure platinum. The whole package is diamond."

Iines's place in the finals was confirmed there and then. Hillary in the blue booth accompanied her. She was a blond and fresh dental nurse from Southampton. Her genitals were almost Brazilian and breasts were firm, slightly smaller than

Iines. Mauro had taken quite a fancy to her rosy appearance.

"Iines and Hillary have been naked so far while you have been fully dressed. Now you have to strip as well."

"It's all right with me."

After a minute naked Mauro emerged from the backstage. Almost immediately their gazes gravitated to his groins doing a check up on his reasonable-sized gear. It was surrounded with bushy pubic hair. Being naked he still was laid back, free and confident. Iines and Hillary complimented his head of hair and tattoos he had revealed after getting undressed.

"Mauro, what is your best feature?" Judith asked.

"Without a doubt my genitals," and grabbed them with both hands.

The ladies applauded.

The crucial moment was on. In Mauro's opinion the situation was really difficult, because both singles were sweet. After a moment of suspense, he ended up choosing Iines. Papparazzi sweated his objective scalding hot, trying to stay away from the camera crew. A Finnish-Italian hug was tender. Mauro justified his choice by telling that Iines had a magnificent body. The Finnish beauty was content.

"My date is very well equipped. It is very impressive that he has an artistic side too."

The game was still on in The Bijou Club. Both wore black. They had a good feeling and they hit it off.

Could this be a start of a beautiful love story?

Iines savoured the thought rotating her cocktail stick in her glass. Right away, tonight she couldn't answer that, she pointed out to the button-eyed inquirer. Mauro lived in Rome and she lived in Helsinki. A long-distance relationship would be a more difficult test than this filming session. Mauro's attitude towards her hesitation was understanding. He stated that our world was getting smaller and smaller and the distance between capitals took only two or three hours.

"One more question, I am Columbo, aren't I?"

Iines almost couldn't contain herself while waiting for his question.

"Do you want to come to my hotel room to have a night cap?"

"Si, signor!"

Iines promised in the spirit of Marilyn Monroe to wear only Chanel 5 in bed. Just visioning it made his trouser front bulge.

When the couple stepped out of the front door the flashlight went on in hypnotic rhythm.

"Thank you! You are so nice and kind! Love conquers every hurdle!" Papparazzi called out behind his camera.

The lovebirds were so smitten with each other that they let him burn film freely.

As Papparazzi watched them leaving he heard Mauro started singing O Sole Mio. The street lights glowed like the sun.

THE MYSTERY OF THE GOLDEN TOILET SEAT

Mandi was having a picnic in maritime Kaivopuisto. It was nice to just hang around on a broad grassland and enjoy tea and cakes. She was reading a detective novel named *Stars Tell Us, Inspector Palmu* written by Mika Waltari, since the book had many substantial confluences with this place. The ambience of past times detective novels excited her. Mandi thought that Waltari should have been concentrating only on these detective novels. The characters were well written and the humour was sassy. Only two of his historical novels were good enough in her opinion, *The Egyptian* and *The Dark Angel*. The latter was better because an elephant had sat on it and thickened the plot more reader-friendly.

On her way back she dropped by Ursa observatory. At Lauri Anttila's *Helios*, a sculpture shaped like a sundial, she saw an unexpected spectacle. On the top of the stone element stood a golden toilet seat. A couple of weeks earlier she had read from internet news that Maurizio Cattelan's million dollar piece called *America* had been stolen from an art exhibition in the UK. The creation displayed a toilet seat made out of 18 carat gold. Had his golden seat emerged in Finland?

Looking more closely she saw that it was only a replica painted with gold paint. The creator of the replica had obviously been inspired by the theft. Mandi took some photos with her mobile phone and sent them to Papparazzi. "On the star rocks of Kaivopuisto I was surprised to see this spectacle. If you can find some use of these photos, be my guest!"

Papparazzi thanked her, asked her to specify the details and made sure that he could sell them using his name. "Are you seriously OK with that?"

Mandi confirmed that she was. "Easy living in Helsinki by night exhibition is taking all my time. Your colleague Iikka Ahtola from *Smirk* is eating all my energy."

Papparazzi understood her situation and added that the highest hill of Kaivopuisto might be a way of earning freelance photographers next paycheque. "The puzzle is not solved yet. I want to catch the perpetrator red handed."

When Papparazzi arrived at the star hill he realized that he had struck out. There was no golden toilet seat on the spot. Those earlier shots didn't fatten his wallet either. The readers had provided a lot of photos of it. They had been published right away. *The Week* had encouraged him to go after the offender. It was easier said than done — the toilet seat was still missing.

One week passed by with no news on the toilet seat front. When there was only a sparkle of hope left the flame flared up again. Papparazzi got wind that the seat had been spotted standing on a landing of the stairs leading up to Uspenski Cathedral. He rushed to the site so fast that his car tyres went oblong. There were a crowd focusing on the toilet seat, but he managed to get shots from various angles. The hands with cameras on were so many that Papparazzi didn't see any chance to sell his photos to any media. There would be excess supply over demand.

Papparazzi went to eat his packed lunch in the nearby

Tove Jansson Park, where he could get a good view of golden cupolas. Nobody was going to get the seat out in broad daylight. It would happen during the evening or night. He had made his way to Kaivopuisto far too late. There was no way he was letting it happen again in Katajanokka. He went to guard the seat at dusk masked as a beggar. An Ikea bag at the bottom of his legs contained his camera gear. In order to enhance his street cred he had brought a sign with a plea: "Beer money, please!"

Some people actually gave him a few coins.

In the early hours there weren't many people around. Mostly he was accompanied by urban animals. A few of them seemed almost desiring to be photographed, but Papparazzi couldn't be bothered. The camera could have blown his cover. The hum of traffic faded away, his eyelids felt heavier, the whole capital was sleeping… He dozed off to the well of sleep. When he started awake after couple of hours, he was terrified to notice that the seat was nowhere to be seen. His head was spinning in disbelief. How on earth could this have happened to him? This nightshift had been a total failure.

Papparazzi's sixth sense told him that this wasn't the end of the seat's story. It had drawn so much attention that the perpetrator must be tempted to continue his escapade even further. Once more he was able to trust his gut feeling. Papparazzi was summoned to Amos's roof domes at the Glass Palace Square. On top of one of them was an all too familiar golden sight. He captured photos like tens of other people and then retreated nearby, waiting and wondering if he could reel in the artist this time. Papparazzi noticed that this time it was set on a vantage point. This might tell a tale about the painter — or not. Standing on guard was a waste of time. At least as long as there was a crowd surrounding it in broad daylight. He decided to go around the Glass Palace and observe the bustle on the streets. At Café Glass Palace he saw briskly striding the former athlete and present visual artist Elli Kokko, pushing a pram, her baby in a kangaroo baby carrier. The hippie-style dressed artist with her daughter was drawing attention from the passers-by. He took photos of the duo. The shots were worth a pittance; a beggar could earn more. Elli was married to musician Hermanni Tuovinen. If the pied piper had accompanied them, the money could have been pouring in. Papparazzi decided to go home at Pikku Huopalahti.

While editing his images Papparazzi got an idea. Why had she taken such a large baby buggy with her? She could have taken a smaller one for her tiny baby. You could hide a toilet seat in those! Top on, blanket over an unnoticeable vehicle was ready for action. Was he getting to the end of a very important lead here? He googled her present exhibitions. At the coming weekend her next expo called Patch of Colour was opening in Gumbostrand Konst & Form. In the homepage of Art Centre was an advertisement saying that the art work focused on light, colour and romance. The scale of feelings stretched from joy to sorrow and fear to disappointment. Papparazzi quickly buried his plans of going to night watch downtown. He already had something better in mind.

He left at first light. He whipped his Kia to K. Hartwall's old industrial milieu in Sipoo. The Centre was not open, so he passed time listening to the radio. He took an occasional stroll in the scenic environment. People went in and out infrequently. Nobody paid attention to him. Black hood wrapped around the scenery. One second felt like a minute, an hour was eternity. He felt slumberous, but he wasn't going to let his eyelids drop.

He was alerted when headlights pierced the surrounding darkness. A van pulled into the courtyard and packed up to the front entrance. A female and a male stepped out of the van stretching their arms and legs. He recognized them as being the artistic couple Kokko & Tuovinen. After they had opened both the front door of the house and the back door of the van Papparazzi dashed to the couple shouting in the back of his mind like a banshee and flashed his flash fiercely. Their faces appeared astounded when they were lifting a bulk that looked like an artwork. Jackpot! Or was it after all a toilet seat? He couldn't confirm it because the piece of art was carefully wrapped up.

"Paparazzo! What the hell are you doing here?"

"It's Papparazzi! I had a hunch that you are involved in the case of golden toilet seat."

Elli remembered seeing him the day before.

"Are you doing a follow-up on me?"

"Of course I am. According to my source you might be involved in the adventures of the golden seat in the capital."

"What on earth are you talking about?"

Papparazzi gave them a short account and made the bohemians chuckle.

"You are barking up the wrong tree! We have nothing to do with the matter!"

"What are you carrying there? Maybe it is the seat I just mentioned…"

"Nonsense!"

Elli tore the cover just so that the shooter was able to see something snow white glowing underneath.

"We are carrying my plaster cast called *Everyday Hero*. Now move over so we can get it inside."

After they were out of his sight Papparazzi took a peek inside the van's cargo trunk. There were mostly paintings and a few smaller statues. It was plausible: the mystery of the golden seat was yet to be solved. He took some pictures of the sweating couple also in the light-coloured interior. Elli wanted to make sure her daughter Karma's face was not recognizable in the magazine.

It is a standard procedure in Finland. Thank you for your loving response to me being here. These photos complement the ones taken yesterday.

"They are a good advertisement for my exhibition!"

Hermanni had only one condition.

"I see you are wearing a scarf. We founded a new Koktuo label, their scarf would suit you handsomely."

Papparazzi promised to think about it seriously. Before leaving he shook hands with both of them.

One month passed, then another. The dearly missed golden artwork was conspicuous by its absence. Until Papparazzi picked up *Metro* to pass the time riding in a tram. The winner of Kiasma's Superficial Finland had been announced. They were looking for today's national phenomena, transformed into flamboyant art. Their best entries would be featured in expo built in the Museum of Contemporary Art. The public had free entry. Joel Sacred-Mound's piece called the *Golden Bending*. The jury described it as being an insightful and humorous piece, which had got a lot of media attention. It was easy to deduce by the last name of the artist why it had been displayed so high above the ground places. Papparazzi contacted straight away the young artist and arranged to meet him in Kiasma. *The Week* held on their deal of publishing pictures of the artist with the golden toilet seat. The best of them was the one with Joel sitting on the seat having an ambiguous look on his face.

Papparazzi had one question above all others he wanted to have an answer to. How did Joel manage to outwit him in Katajanokka? The explanation was simple. The artist had made a deal in good community spirit with the representatives of Ursa, Uspenski Cathedral and Amos Rex that he could take his artwork on display in Kaivopuisto, Katajanokka and Kamppi. They had shown a green light to the project. As it happened in Uspenski Cathedral that the security guard had seen a wino sleeping near the *Golden Bending*. He thought that he had arrived at the scene for the glitter and to take the seat with him after waking up, so he had recovered it to a more secure place.

"I was notified about it immediately and collected it from the security firm office the same day."

Papparazzi lowered his pants and mooned to Joel, who was flabbergasted.

"Why did you do that?"

"This is my golden bending to you, with all friendship. The wino you saw was me in disguise! I stalked the perpetrator which was you, but I was bitterly disappointed. Guess how many times I have fretted over my screw up!"

"Too bad, undeniably, but our actions were not related back then. Our paths did not cross until now."

Papparazzi acknowledged the statement to be true with his smile. He pulled his pants up and told him that he felt relieved since the mystery of the golden toilet seat had been solved once and for all. He slapped Joel on his shoulder.

"It is time to have cup of coffee honouring your medal."

VEGAN SLIPPED!

Papparazzi moved the orange canvas aside on the Market Square and targeted Finland's best-known player on vegan stage Iiro Onnela. He had a straight line of vision on the other market stall behind it, where the raw vegan diet follower sat. He had announced that he had left out of his diet meat, fish and dairy products. There were a large number of fans following Iiro's blog and social media updates. Now he was munching salmon and French fries with a healthy appetite. Shoots were stored in steady pace. Papparazzi checked them on the camera display and noted that the diner's expression touched heaven in some of them. It was apparent there was an air of captivating danger and attraction of forbidden fruit. One aphorism of Mark Twain popped into the photographer's mind. "Adam was human: he didn't want the apple just for sake of it — he wanted it because it was forbidden."

It was obvious that no additional photos were required, so the camera hero padded away.

Thursday brought along *The Week* where Iiro ate salmon with delight on the cover page. The main headline screamed: "Vegan slipped!" His indiscretion was trashed in the inner pages thoroughly. They also called Iiro for a comment. He apologized for the incident. He still believed in a vegetable-based diet, but he had to add fish and eggs due to health problems. He had also had indigestion. The fact he regretted mostly was that he hadn't himself shared the changes the doctor had ordered him with his followers and business partners. He took responsibility for his actions solely. Thursday was full of hopelessness to him.

The storm broke out in social media; people lashed out at the star. He was claimed to tarnish the whole vegan lifestyle and his doctrine collapsed. He was accused of lying to everybody. Veg policewomen Niina and Jasmin told him in their YouTube video to piss off. This would also happen to all other vegans who were proved to be just after big profits. Veg cops put among other things a live perch on a hot frying pan to stew. "Use your own brains and stop believing in gurus."

Thousands of followers vanished from Iiro's channels in a few days. His parents changed their pages from public to private, because they couldn't stand crushing criticism targeted at their son. Iiro was also told to get lost from social media quietly. He wasn't ready to do that; instead he took a defence battle on healthy lifestyle. Food was not such a dominant issue anymore.

The toughest breakers around the commotion died down in time. However, not completely. Pipsa Korpela's *Sleepover* show, visiting at Iiro's — Papparazzi's victim — home, took care of that. On the programme listing his name was written right, that is, there was a double-p in the middle.

"That proves you are renowned in your field," Machine appraised at Papparazzi's home, where he had entered to watch the show.

"I wish my face won't be worn too much. That will, if anything, make my work more difficult. I have to wear disguises more often and mask myself with hairpiece and false beard. Me not liking it at all!"

The broadcast started. Getting to know the apartment and the designated person. Before long came the moment when Iiro got the chance to open up the Fishgate that rocked the whole state. He had surfed on a wave crest of prosperity until Papparazzi had taken photos by fish platter. Its coming out had hit him hard, pushing him to the brink of a nervous breakdown. Lucrative partnership agreements had terminated like hitting a brick wall. He had started a mixed diet. That was another thing he could blame Papparazzi for. Explanations after another. Iiro had his voice heard. Nobody had invited Papparazzi to the show or asked his comments on the matter.

They were singing from a completely different song in a one-bedroom flat in Pikku Huopalahti. What do you mean by calling yourself a victim? Iiro had enjoyed his salmon in a public place in broad daylight. Everyone present had seen it — and Papparazzi had captured it.

They turned off the telly at that point, where Pipsa strutted to the breakfast table wearing crumbled pyjamas.

Machine toasted and raised the spirit by blurting:

"There is no point in dwelling on this, that could spoil the whole evening. A shot will dissolve the wrinkles."

Seven days after the broadcast the photographer bumped into Iiro downtown. When he recognized the shooter he froze, turned heels and bolted onto the other side of the street. Why? What was in the man's mind? Papparazzi let the ex-vegan go on his way. He asked himself once again who had tarnished Iiro's squeaky clean public image. Was it him or Iiro Onnela himself munching his forbidden fruit in Market Square?

GETTING RID OF SPAWNING BARRIERS

Papparazzi was lunching in Restaurant Tilkanranta. He sat in a circular beer garden eating his pepper steak. The sun dazzled his eyes. It was peaceful, only a few regulars drinking their beers at the nearby tables. He had become very familiar with him over the years. After moving to Helsinki, he had visited Tilkankatu number 6 more frequently, these days not so often. The ambiance in there was bohemian and carefree — at weekends even wild.

He knew some of the boozers' first names. Currently old hands Veke and Lefa were sipping their beers. The turnover rate was pretty fast among the staff, so he didn't have many nodding acquaintances in the place.

Mostly he did have smooth conversations with an Estonian called Gerli and an Iraqi called Firas. Papparazzi hadn't seen them in a while. He took his after lunch free coffee with him in a paper cup and shifted to have a seat in a park bench in Tilkantori. There were some down-and-out people making deals. Bundles, cigarette packs and bottles were slipped into plastic bags. Chats were seasoned with swear words.

Papparazzi wasn't quite sure if a couple of boozers were weighing him with their gazes. At first, he didn't allow it to disturb his cosy time, but after they started to motion towards him, he got excited. As if they were drawing straws, whether they dared to approach him or not. Finally, they gathered their courage to come with a wobble to him and present their matter:

"Aren't you that shooter of celebs?"

Papparazzi stated the fact and introduced himself to them; their names were Bojo and Jiri. The lads were youngish, with dishevelled appearances. Scars and dark under eyes on their faces told that they had attended the school of life the hard way.

"We have a shooting tip to you on the condition that you open your wallet."

The request aroused a healthy suspicion in Papparazzi's mind. Only he wasn't sure how much cash he was carrying. Possibly none. Before opening his wallet, he wanted to know what uses they wanted the money for.

"You're not going to use it to buy some firewater?"

"Of course not! We are going to buy some stodge. We have been listening to our empty tummies groaning for hours."

There we have it! Papparazzi pulled his wallet from his back pocket. There was only twenty euros in it. He waved the note in front of their faces and pressured them:

"Tip first, note second!"

"We have been here for hours pondering what people there are hanging around at the outlet of the Haaga Brook. We have seen all kinds of Mr Suits and glamour-pusses, but mostly camouflaged swaggerers."

"So, what! Why would they be any interest of mine?"

Jiri, the blonder of the duo, paused for a second before revealing a secret.

"One of the swaggerers is… film star Jesse Pyykkö!"

Tilkantori Information Agency's news relay excited

Papparazzi — on the condition that the information was valid.

"Are you sure?"

The men nodded.

"We know and recognize this bad boy of the movie world."

Papparazzi shadowed his eyes with his hand and scanned forward in order to see the crowd by the waterway. There was a noticeably big buzz going on. For once he was able to take pictures in his own backyard! The note changed hands and the photographer zipped to grab his tools.

Papparazzi was gazing on a bridge across the brook. There were parties on both sides of the river, talking lively based on their flailing hands. It took some time before he noticed a popular actor who blended into the green nature in his green anorak. The distance between them was only about a hundred metres. Papparazzi stashed his binoculars into his jacket pocket, put his camera on a tripod and started to snap pictures. The rhythm was slow, because he just wanted to catch the brown-haired and moustached actor on the pictures.

After about fifteen minutes Jesse noticed and started stepping towards him. Papparazzi increased his pace of shooting.

"Hi! What are you doing?"

"What do you think?"

According to Jesse this was quite a private gathering, where no media representatives were invited. There were only some authorities and environmentalists. He was introduced to a new organic creek bed. He compared the incident to having somebody gatecrashing a party in somebody's home.

"How did you manage to come here with your long tube?"

"I can smell celebs from distance."

After hearing his answer the star's stiff facial impression changed to be more positive. After hearing that the photos would end up in *The Week*, he started to calculate the advantages in his mind. He had practically made up his mind to contribute some money for conservation of fish stocks in Haaga Brook. The passionate fisherman wanted to do his part in easing trouts' and other possible sea-goers' spawning journey.

"My five digits donation has not been officially published. Because I appreciate a reporter's footwork, *The Week* will get this scoop."

Papparazzi thanked him with a bow. He gave him Isto Luodikko's contact information.

"Call Isto as soon as possible, so he can draw up a swinging text of this cordial subject."

On return to Tilkantori information about the subject was overflowing from Jesse's mouth.

"The most important rise barrier that is the dam will be dismantled from the outlet and a subsection will be built as a natural closure to a new place. Small-scale upgrades to the riverbed are being done by volunteers. I am also volunteering. Visible results will be accomplished in a few years time. Haaga Brook will be lively and full of life."

They arrived at the citybike station. And who was waiting for the greenie there? The Thai-Portuguese model beauty Malee Oliveira! Jesse and Malee had been lovers for a long time. They had also attended The Independence Day Ball in President's Castle. The camera was having a wild ride and *The Week* had another sensational spawning story.

A TIGHT SPOT IN EPILÄ

Papparazzi was spooning his cereal in the breakfast room in Hotel Haapalinna. He enjoyed his breakfast in peace reading the newspaper and watching news on the wall-mounted TV. Besides him there were one family with kids, a few labourers and a middle-aged man apparently suffering polydipsia. The staff had to fill up the water jug continuously.

A frisky man from Pikku Huopalahti had come there to spend the weekend in Tampere. Vapriikki exhibitions, Market Hall and Amurin Helmi were regular parts of his travel plan. This time he had also explored Ratina Shopping Mall, which turned out being a size too big for his liking.

The atmosphere in the breakfast room electrified when ebony star rapper Lemo stepped in. He had hidden his woolly hair resembling a flocked carpet under a retro cap. He had his sunglasses on as always. Jewellery glittered around his neck and fingers. He held his hand gently on the shoulder of a Latino lady. Her head reached barely up to his belly button while wearing high-heeled shoes. Papparazzi took for granted that they had booked themselves a spacious combo with sauna. He himself boarded a single room.

Then it dawned on Papparazzi. Didn't he just the week before last read from some women's magazine how happy Lemo was with his Fenno-Swedish wife Brita? The story was run in the couple's home, wardrobes had been opened and gilded memories. The rapper had been asked to evaluate everything he was wearing, including clothes and jewellery. The cost of his whole ensemble was almost 100, 000 euros. The mere cost of his Rolex watch was over 30, 000 euros. He was wearing a solid gold Day-Date model i.e. The President. It was nicknamed after the fact that it was the favourite model of the presidents of the United States. Brita and Lemo were so madly in love that nothing could separate them. Ever.

Papparazzi's ears and eyes were more than decoration. He saw the star's hands were moving like octopus tentacles on the dark-haired woman's back and bottom, when they were serving themselves on the buffet with something to bite and hot beverages. He heard how grateful the warbler was of the fun they had the previous night. The broad sneered.

They sat down at the table next to him. Lemo was not really hungry, he mostly fumbled with his mobile phone. The damsel had a healthy appetite. She talked endlessly about her makeup and her friends. The star had a sugary expression on his face. It was hard to say whether he hummed to the view on the screen or his chick's chatter. In the evening he had a gig in Ilona Night Club. The lady would stay put in the hotel. The rapper lowered his voice and emphasized that their secret affair should not come out to third parties. Officially the sex bomb was the star's personal assistant.

Revealing secrets was in Papparazzi's blood. The camera bag was in his car trunk, so practically his mobile phone was his only means available for taking photos at breakfast. The secret lovers could leave the premises at any moment. Would he reveal himself or should he stake out at the car park? As painful it was, he leaned towards the latter.

Papparazzi signed out of the hotel a day early. Staying

there would have been utterly impossible, potentially threatening his health and well-being. He fetched his camera from the Kia and stayed near the front door and the stairs to watch out for his prey. He had to spend countless hours peeking behind the bushes. He even fished out the name of Lemo's companion: Celia Ribas. The Spanish girl had worked as a right hand for the last six months.

Eventually the shooter in the bush got lucky. The couple came out into the open entangled with each other and kissing. He captured their pecking just before the lovey-doves noticed him, startled and pulled out. The photo shoot went on. Celia and Lemo started a commotion.

"What, what? Can't you be left alone even in Epilä?"

Although the secret lovebirds buzzed in an antsy manner around him, he remained composed and introduced himself. The camera was shut off.

"I am just doing my job."

"You took pictures of us and make money with our assistance. Stinking bastard!"

Celia was more reconciling and tried to bargain with him over the shoots.

"How much would it cost if you just removed them in front of us?"

Papparazzi refused her proposal. Lemo said that he could easily break the camera and the photographer's jaw at will. He would not do that because he was a smoker of a peace pipe. Papparazzi was able to pull himself from his predicament. The couple stood staring at him with their mouths open.

The pictures decorated the covers of yellow press next week. They went also on international distribution, since Lemo rapped in English. His career was taking a rapid take off around the world, since he had already conquered Finland. He got more material to his songs from his divorce and his new hot romance. Papparazzi was also mentioned in his new production, in a chorus of his song Stinking Shit.

"Papparazzi, you are hanging in my butt like a mongrel! I am bleeding, throwing up. I am so tired of you. You are just stinking shit!"

SMILE, YOU'RE ON CAMERA

Topi Salokannel took a peek at his wristwatch in the back seat of a cab. Minutes had passed painstakingly laborious, but now — at 8 pm — showtime struck. He paid for the trip and stepped out of the car with his wife Jenni in front of Treffi Pub & Bistro in Herttoniemi. Both of them were dressed in their better clothes.

Tension was rippling in the air. They knew that something unusual was about to happen soon. Suddenly the flashes started to blink from multiple fronts blinding their eyes. The windows of the suburban pub glittered.

"Say cheese!"

"Look here!"

"Smile, you're on camera!"

Passers-by dug up their mobile phone and started to snap pictures of the couple. They must be somebody famous. *The Week* might pay good money for these reader photos. Further away they heard somebody shouting:

"Leave them alone!"

Papparazzi, Mandi and Machine turned a deaf ear and went on banging.

Topi and Jenni, both working in the financial sector, had booked Papparazzi with his sidekicks on site to celebrate the missus expecting their first child. The couple radiated through the photo session.

"Darling! You have deserved all this attention and publicity."

Inside the pub were waiting proverbial cheeseburgers along with *The Week*'s reporter Maria Paananen.

Topi and Jenni had booked a Day Celebrity package, which was Papparazzi's new line of business. *The Week* wanted to report it first to all the people. With Papparazzi photos. The reporter congratulated them on their upcoming blessed event i.e. the birth of their firstborn. The little munchkin would come out in six months.

"Do you have any other reason to take part in this kind of media game?"

They revealed being of a generation accustomed to being in the pictures. It was an important part of their parties and everyday life. Papparazzi with his sidekicks was something they have never experienced — that is until now.

"How did it feel like to get out of the cab as a celebrity couple?"

"Amazing! It was something unique and we felt special. The reactions of people walking in the street were baffling."

"A day as a celebrity costs thousands. Is the price worth your while?"

"Let's put it this way, it is true that the final invoice is grim, but it is something we are prepared to take care of. In return we get a unique thrill and a photo montage."

Jenni's and Topi's package tour had started off a couple of hours earlier in a hair salon. When the hair was well i.e. all was well, they had been captured in their first photos. The second place of strike was in a bistro quarter in Herttis. The trio shot as the interview was held when they were dining. At night they were being photographed arriving at GLO Hotel

Kluuvi. Next day the photo sessions were due to continue on the streets of the inner city. In the evening *The Week* would ask their comments of the day by phone.

Maria had asked her very last question already in Herttoniemi.

"Could you imagine the ongoing publicity?"

"Twenty-four hours of this treat is quite enough."

"Today was one of most thrilling of our lives. We will be looking back to it sitting in our rocking chairs!"

ON THE TRAIL OF A WORK DODGER

Waiting time was terribly long in a car parked along Rusthollarintie. Papparazzi was snooping the ideologically unemployed Ville Etola to return at the crack of dawn. Finland's objector to work had rented a flat from a redbrick apartment building.

Passers-by were staring at the wheels. Some of them were undoubtedly wondering what he was doing day in and day out. He couldn't budge, since he had got wind that Ville might really go to work every day.

The photographer had already had time to explore the ideas of the East Helsinki resident. Ville encouraged people to step out of the treadmill and do things that they felt more meaningful to themselves. Being a paid employee had reached the end of the road. Industrial action against the Job Centre. Over a decade ago he had made the term shitwork a talk of the town. He categorized that work in burger joints and labour hire companies were good examples of it.

A cab zoomed past and Papparazzi caught a glimpse of Ville sitting on the back seat. He took a tight U-turn chasing the cabby. The traffic was fast-paced and traffic lights turned on high speed. The newspaper photographer stayed close, but never licked the rear bumper. They came to Itis in a row. Shadowing continued on foot inside the mall in the R-kioski based along the main corridor. Ville rushed to the back room and re-entered behind the counter in a black turtleneck T-shirt. Well, there he was — working in sales. An intense contrast between words and acts.

Papparazzi stayed in the main corridor deliberating his shooting options. R-kioski owners had very strict rules on taking photos inside their premises. This time he had a rucksack on his back. In addition to his camera gear, he had packed a change of clothes for the situations when he needed a disguise. He went to the nearest men's room and dressed up as a foreign tourist. His wig was raven black, his glasses had thick frames and his false moustache resembled Super Mario. A linen shirt and jeans complemented his casual look.

He strolled around the kiosk, read magazines and praised Finland and the colourfulness of the space speaking bad English with an Indian accent. Staff behind the counter concluded that he was a harmless foreign chap. Once Ville's attention was focused fully on customer serving, the masked man grabbed his camera phone and snapped pictures at a slow pace in a way that showed the salesperson's face leaving customers out of the picture. Now and then Papparazzi took selfies. He got some exposures of Ville positioning tabloids on the newspaper stand on the corridor. They exchanged a few words about their covers; after that he escaped the scene.

The catch of the photos was good, but he couldn't cook up a main story. Besides, Papparazzi had heard speculations that Ville held another job elsewhere. The next few days passed following his movements, mostly in Puotila. The guru lived according to his teaching and avoided working. Just as despair was sneaking in, the cab arrived at Ville's neighbourhood. Step on it and follow him. The destination was at Distribution Company's Finnish branch in Vantaa. After half an hour he was messing his bang cock in plain view. He was pedalling the tail right behind him.

His distribution circuit was in Pähkinärinne. Getting closer to the northern shopping mall Papparazzi accelerated in front of his prey and parked his car. He stormed out, the camera in his hand, and lifted it up in front of Ville wearing his work clothes. Photos were hitting.

Ville froze to gaze in awe of the situation he was in. Papparazzi told him who he was and what he was doing.

"I could never have imagined to get a photographer like you after me. This is a great honour!"

"How come? You are working, aren't you, although you are not supposed to. It contradicts everything you are preaching."

Ville told him that he had been mentally prepared for a while that someday he would be caught having a job. He had done locum in different places quite a long time now.

"Why?"

"Because of hunger."

Living unemployed he was ready to face the curses of publicity holding his head high, if Papparazzi could give him a hundred euros in return. They sealed the deal with a handshake.

The only way of surviving this is humour. That disguise of yours was well-played, Papparazzi. You passed with flying colours playing your role in Itis.

Papparazzi took a bow with attributable value.

In *Smirk* they got excited. Now they had enough material for a big story. After its publication Ville wound up attacked in social media. He was a regular guest in current affairs TV shows. The ideologically unemployed also stood for election to the Parliament, but his number of votes was too low.

Smirk's editor-in-chief Ilkka Ahtola phoned. A story titled "The work is a sequence of dyskinesia caused by hunger" had broken records in sales. He invited the photographer to the editorial office to honour the accomplishment with cake and coffee. More such stories!

IT'S THE FINAL MOPDOWN!

There was a real razzmatazz going on in K-Supermarket Herkkupata in Siilinjärvi. Coffee and cake event thrown to celebrate 92 million Euro Jackpot winners. The jackpot had brought 50 new millionaires into the county. The waiting lines at the service point stretched on to the street. In the sale point of the victorious pool game was also Papparazzi mixing business and pleasure. He was at the forefront with his camera when the merchant Jyrki Huttunen started serving cake. Farm owners with their caps on the heads and their missuses dressed elegantly for the occasion spooned the berry delicacy into their mouths.

Everybody in the village knew well which ones were among the winners. Some of them were probably in the pictures Papparazzi had taken but in very Finnish manner they had kept their good fortunes hidden. Papparazzi took photos to *Evening Paper*, reporter Liisa Ukkola inquired of the feelings of the locals. At a general level everybody was happy for those who had taken part in the pool. It was believable that the reality could turn into a fairy tale in a flash. Some of them had seen the list of the pool the previous week, but hadn't taken part in it. Now they regretted it.

Papparazzi had not been alerted to the spot just to see people eating the victory cake. *Evening Pape*r had done some basic work in order to get a personal interview from a freshly made millionaire. Cleaner Inkeri Tahvanainen was known with certainty as being one of the lucky. She had given it a serious thought, but she wanted a kick-ass fee for her troubles. The only thing Papparazzi knew about the negotiations was that her figure had more than four digits in it before she opened her mouth. At times he got notes from the editor's office that it was far easier to get an interview from the Pope than this lady. At the end they agreed to meet. Scoop, cover and spread on the weekend issue, please!

The couple from *Evening Paper* went on to Restaurant Backpack Man; they had booked a snug for the summit. They were well catered for, especially with alcohol. The newspaper picked up the tab.

During the meal Papparazzi sensed Inkeri's trepidation. The thin brunette clenched her hands, fiddled with the tablecloth and napkins and adjusted her specs back and forth. The only reason she had for this was that she was taking a hike from this neighbourhood as soon as possible to live in a luxurious residence in downtown Helsinki. The switch would be easy since she had a rented flat at the moment. In the capital nobody would recognize her, which would stop people prying about what she was going to do with her fortune.

Liisa turned her recorder on after they finished their meal. She wanted to salvage every word. Her nickname was Liisa Recorder. She got her name after she had been forced to interview a businessman she detested. She had led him to the Press Café in the publishing house and left him there alone talking to the recorder. She went back after an hour to retrieve her widget after the businessman was long gone. There was no history of what kind of story she had created out of it. Her immediate boss had given her an earful — and her new nickname.

Inkeri loosened up at that point when their desserts were served. Her words just started pouring out.

"At first, I just couldn't believe that I had just won a jackpot of millions. I still have a hard time understanding that it will end up in my bank account. I am afraid that this is just a dream."

Money symbolised her being free and able to make her dreams come true.

"What other things are you going to purchase than the condo?"

"A new shopping bag at least. Probably some expensive impulse buys. I am going to travel a lot too."

A cruise around the world was her number one wish. She had only visited resorts in Spain and Greece at this point.

"Presumably I will spend my winters in Fuengirola. I can get along there speaking only Finnish."

She had already figured out that a couple of millions wasn't enough to fulfil all her dreams.

Living in this world can be expensive.

Liisa Recorder asked the waiter to get them more drinks for her interviewee and started to tackle her personal history. She was a divorcee with no kids. All her life she had resided in Siilinjärvi and done similar jobs. Until the Big Bang she would have been able to retire in three years. Now she was on the countdown on her last days at work.

Papparazzi was painfully aware of the fact that he needed to get more pictures of Inkeri. He asked if it was possible to shoot her at work as a cleaner. She waved a bunch of keys in front of them.

"Why not? I have access to many companies here."

Inkeri suggested that they should go to Hairdressing Salon Harlekiini; they would be closing at six pm in Alexis Center. The place would be peaceful about an hour after closing time. Liisa Recorder stated on her part that she had a plane to catch in Kuopio Airport. The return flight to Helsinki was due to leave in a couple of hours.

"I will finish my story of the coffee and cake event in Herkkupata in the plane. It has to be in tomorrow's paper. I have the photos already."

Papparazzi nodded as confirmation.

The Lucky Inkeri story was something that the reporter could work on more thoroughly; her deadline on that was looming a few days ahead. She bid her farewell to Papparazzi and his shooting subject, who ordered stiff drinks and sparklers. And their second, third, fourth even. Their words started to go backwards at the point where they were heading to the shopping centre.

When they reached their destination, they started off working. Although Inkeri had taken her equipment out of the closet a thousand times before, this was the first time she did it hammered. Papparazzi felt himself being boozy.

Chairs, job carts, sinks, mirrors and waiting sofas, all got cleansing treatment with flash blazing. She reached the best level A using her hoover and mop. While washing she threw a fandango. Papparazzi found the sight so amusing that he swirled down on the moist and glossy floor his butt first. He continued shooting from frog perspective.

The guard emerged in the salon accompanied by the suit. Inkeri knew both of them only too well. The man in uniform was Taisto Heiskanen and the other guy was the cleaner's boss Santeri Jääskeläinen.

"What on earth are you doing here?"

"As you can see: working our asses off!"

Papparazzi introduced himself and explained that he was illustrating a personal story of Inkeri, the hero of the clean up; it was going to be published in *Evening Paper*. The bigwig raised his finger.

"Although this is a good and welcomed cause, its way of implementation is inadequate. You should have asked permission for the shooting beforehand."

He continued steaming off.

"What is this smell? Couldn't be alcohol, could it?"

"It is just disinfectant," Inkeri answered with dry laughter.

Mr Necktie didn't believe her; he insisted that his employee should be breathalyzed. Inkeri's temper boiled over. She stormed to her boss and struck her cleaning gear into his hand.

"Hereby and this instant I state my resignation! It's the final mopdown!"

Inkeri captured Papparazzi under her arm; then they left the scene with a stumble. The guard and the nob followed them with flabbergasted gazes.

After the runner they had an afterparty, where else than in Restaurant Backbag Man. Flashbacks of the night were so fragmented and foggy that they didn't go over the publication threshold.

A JOLLY GOOD FELLOW

Duo Ramshackle had driven to Järvenpää by nightfall. Machine's car had almost seized up a couple of times due to frosty weather, but they had solved their problems using their wits. The owner of Jamppa K-Market Marko Hoikkaniemi reported his desperate situation to Machine and Papparazzi while they were all standing near the cash desks. Shoplifters and thieves had targeted the grocery store. He had notified the police of these misdemeanours, but they had not led anywhere due to the anonymity of the light fingers. Now his cup had spilled over. From now on, starting tonight, he was going to run after every shoplifter heading to the hills. That's why he had summoned Papparazzi to the scene. The merchant was delighted that the famous photographer had taken his sidekick to tag along.

"Goods were taken with hundred percent reduction daily. There is no doubt in my mind that it will happen in the next few hours. You will certainly get footage that will interest the media."

Papparazzi was staking out near the cash registers; Machine stalked in his car at the car park. He had parked it in close proximity of the main entrance. They both had their cameras within arm's reach.

Salesman Kaius Taavitsainen was set nearest to Papparazzi. During quieter periods, he shared his horror stories. Shoplifters were picking particularly the most expensive groceries like meat, cheese and booze. In addition to beer runners he had met some masked robbers.

"Sometimes they come to haunt in my dreams. It would be a good thing if we could raise awareness of this issue and reduce the number of flippant customers. Fear is the worst part of this job."

They had done quite a deal. The staff increased camera surveillance and paid attention to the placement of goods. The most expensive goods were sold just over the counter. Some of the perpetrators were banned from the premises.

When they started to talk about the consequences of the shoplifters' actions the shop owner joined in the conversation and laughed heartily.

"Practically the crooks do it without any retribution whatsoever. They might get a fine which they have no intention of paying."

Hours passed without incident. It was intriguing to watch Kaius at work. His service attitude was on the spot. Thank you, you're welcome, have a nice day and see you soon echoed from his mouth intermittently. The customers had different kinds of reactions. Some just went silently to the end of the conveyer belt to bag their shopping. Others chattered more than their share.

Shortly before the closing time a youngster in shabby winter clothes emerged at the till. His red beanie was pulled down on the head and a muffler covered the lower part of his face. Only his sweet potato nose peeked out properly. Something shiny bobbed up in his hand. He demanded the salesman to hand over all the cash from the till. A stickup! Papparazzi dashed to shoot the incident. He captured a sequence of photos of Kaius stuffing money into a bag the crook had handed him. Papparazzi saw from the corner of his eye another youngster running to the front exit with a couple of 12 packs of beer in his arms. The shop owner tried to stop the ragged guy wearing a fur hat, but he pushed him aside. In the meantime, his accomplice grabbed the money bag from Kaius and rushed out with his after his pal. He dodged the shopkeeper's attempt to tackle him. The retailer got up agilely and left off to run after them. After 100 metres' sprint the man in a vest caught up with them.

The shopkeeper was a head taller than the delinquents and attempted to use his size and weight to stop their flight going on. The beers fell on the ground. Machine arrived in time to witness with his piece of shooting equipment how the beanie man whacked the shopkeeper straight in his face with his fist. The strike broke his specs and sent them flying in a pile of snow nearby. Yanking, pulling, holding, chokeholds, grunting, puffing and cursing. Now Papparazzi was also strobing his flashlight to the fighters. By a miracle, the crooks managed to let themselves loose with the money loot. The thirst quenchers they left willingly behind.

The shopkeeper groaned on the ground while Papparazzi shot close-ups. The crook chaser's eyes were swollen and red, so he predicted that he would resemble a panda the next day. Although his nose had taken a few hits, nothing was broken. Teeth seemed to be intact.

"It doesn't matter that it hurts. I'll be chasing those crooks in the future."

It was about the time when Machine was able to show how gifted a runner he was. That was the reason why Papparazzi had taken him to this gig. They had drawn up a plan for this kind of scenario. Although it had been unlikely, this time it had just come true. Machine left his camera to Papparazzi and sprinted after the runners. Shortly he was breathing in their necks in Wärtsilänkatu. They ran in a row about one kilometre, until the scruffy guys' steps started to burden. It became obvious to them that they couldn't shake the marathoner. They stopped and Machine persuaded them to go back to the end zone. At that point the lads seemed surprisingly co-operative and tame. They showed Machine their loot — only about a hundred euros — and also their instrument they used to threaten the seller. It was a paper cutter.

When the walkers returned to the scene the police picked the suspects up to put away. Papparazzi along with other media people hovered around. The hero's glory was enjoyed by Marko Hoikkaniemi along with Machine. On next day's TV broadcasts the latter told that since he had taken the trouble to travel all the way to Järvenpää, he had simply got the urge to fight for the good guys. He could have run a longer time if needed. He had just done his civic duty.

The most memorable moment was seen in the winter night when a mixed congregation gathered in front of the shop and tuned a song to good guys: "For he's a jolly good fellow…" Even the unknown composer of the song would have wiped tears from his eyes.

PAPPARAZZI IN LOVE

Papparazzi was running towards the front entrance of MTV3's main building in Ilmalankatu. He got a glimpse of pop singer Alma hopping inside a taxicab. She had been the star guest in *Good Morning Finland* TV show. As soon as Papparazzi had seen ads that the Miss Yellow Hair was going to be in the show, he had dashed to mobilize himself. The spoon and a pat of butter had been left in the middle of oatmeal porridge on a plate. He had also left his coffeemaker on. Luckily it would be switching off automatically in a few minutes from now.

A female voice got in his ears.

"You're too late!"

He turned over to see who had made the comment. An almond-eyed brunette, stylishly dressed and made-up female photographer raised her camera proudly.

There are tens of pictures of Alma hidden inside this.

Although he was annoyed with the matter, these things happened from time to time. When bad karma hit him, it happened frequently. Papparazzi had noticed the joyful lady previously. Now it was high time to get better acquainted.

"Everybody knows you as Papparazzi, so I cannot be anything but Mammarazzi."

Papparazzi was surprised.

"I'll be damned! I could not imagine in my tiny little mind that I was going to bump into my female counterpart, let alone having a similar pet name."

"I must confess straight away that I just made it up. You don't object, do you?"

"Not in the least! It feels more like an honorary gesture!"

"Good to hear!"

They went through the Alma case with smiles on their faces.

"Alma was good-tempered and her attitude to shooting was one of a woman of the world. She even gave me her autograph and a couple of comments."

There wouldn't be others fishing on the same ground since the pop musician was due to take a morning flight from Helsinki-Vantaa to London.

Mammarazzi was going to tender out magazines and sell exclusively to the highest bidder. They both agreed that she could make a fortune out of them.

They hugged goodbye. The squeeze took long enough to be something other than just friendly. Was it an infatuated hug? Was Papparazzi thinking too highly? Mammarazzi's ring finger was empty. Why should he be paying attention to that?

While driving home he recalled Mammarazzi's real name. It was Elisa Maininki. The forty-year-old female photographer worked mostly for women's magazines. Her shots were published in *Pirkka* on a regular basis. In any case rap artist Mikael Gabriel, Formula One driver Kimi Räikkönen's wife Minttu Räikkönen, singer Suvi Teräsniska and TV star Arman Alizad had been targeted by her. Alma had also been on the cover. He whizzed a text message to Mammarazzi about it. The answer came promptly: "This is for your eyes only! I took the pictures of Alma for *Pirkka*. We exchanged our contact details then. And yes: Alma invited me to meet her at the Owl Valley.

Good detective work by the way!"

Papparazzi's lips curved into a smile when he sent a sunny smiley to thank her for the confidential information.

The field of paparazzi was very masculine. All the most valuable paparazzi photos were taken by pairs of trousers. It was as obvious that the female stars appeared in them — mostly they had very little on. There were also mamarazzi — and one Mammarazzi — in the picture nowadays. Pappparazzi thought this as being a healthy progression. Women had still a lot to give in this field.

Pappararazzi threw a glimpse over his shoulder. Love had been a lonely rider on the back seat. The window of opportunity for romances had not opened. He had had his calendar full 24/7. He looked at the seat of the assistant driver and saw Mammarazzi. It was just an illusion, but the picture shimmered in his mind. Was he, against all odds, smitten?

The couple made lengthening phone calls to each other. Elisa had a two-bedroom rental near Shopping Mall Tripla. She was also a divorcee. Secondary school aged son Ilkka lived alternate weeks with his parents. The anchor of Love Boat was let loose for good when Papparazzi's hand gravitated to Mammarazzi's hand in the moonlight on Tilkantori. They had left behind dancing on tables in Tilkanranta and headed towards their rosy future. A wonderful, tingling night was completed in fulfilment in Papparazzi's bedroom in his flat.

The time passed in a daze. Social visits, dinners, cultural activities and a whole array of photos. The most suggestive ones were taken in Mansion Park Tullivuori using the timer: they were naked, tightly closed together; thus no strategic parts were shown. They had made sure that there were no extra people in sight. The set was also sheltered, bounded by hedges.

They had just got their clothes on when an old man with his aide pushing his rollator emerged in sight. Later that night a pine cone was flattened under their backs inside a trekking tent.

Elisa had a good heart and warm sense of humour. She was all ears when there was something important to tell. Her voice was soft and vibrant. Papparazzi could have listened to her reading the phonebook for hours on end. He was willing to follow her to the end of the world. He was so in love with her up to his scarf.

They draped to disguise as different characters. Papparazzi walked in the street in a gentlemanly outfit waggling a flashy cane. Mammarazzi was the spitting image of Paris Hilton. Her peak performance was dressing up in an army green gillie suit and blended in the terrain so well in Tilkanniitty that Papparazzi failed to find her. They bought cameras masked as cigarette packs and lighters from a wed store. Someday they might come in handy in real life. They hid spy cameras in each other's flats. Papparazzi found one from his fire detector, Mammarazzi from an innocent looking screw hole.

They also had fun taking pictures when they were on action. The most hilarious incidents were those taken when they were doing mamarazzo and paparazzo gigs consequently. These were very valuable memories for their own albums.

They played with light and shadows. That's what taking photographs is all about.

The best things ever were the joint celebrity hunts, with shared profits. From the backstage of *Ice Hockey Love* TV show they got pictures of ex-player Teemu Selänne and his wife Sirpa together. Crime drama was met when they got to

Restaurant Wiskari where its owners, singer and songwriter Arttu Wiskari and his wife Pauliina, were investigating the signs of the light fingered after a burglary. They also captured minister Pekka Haavisto kissing his spouse Antonio Flores on the stairs of Parliament House. Mammarazzi managed to get a picture that looked like they were kissing passionately, when it actually was just a light kiss.

Mammarazzi and Papparazzi were also able to go through the trash bag of a porn star Tupsu who was well known for her turbo lips and silicone breast implants. The most interesting pieces of garbage were put together and photographed. Beer and soda bottles, cans, cereal boxes, leftover fast food, torn gift wrappers, wrinkly envelopes and magazines, bread bags, milk and washing powder cartoons and a remote control were all neatly placed on a dark background. The artistic impression of it was so classy that *Esari* newspaper published an art critic's evaluation of it. The headline of the story was "So plastic it makes me sick". The world would drown in its own shit if everybody lived like Tupsu. The sex bomb was devastated. How did Mammarazzi and Papparazzi get their hands on trash taken inside a locked space? The operation took a lot of patience and professional skills. In *Smirk* Tupsu lifted her middle finger and swore revenge on the camera clowns.

Along with the media attention Mandi booked Mammarazzi expo time in Gallery Papparazzi. The opening of Best of Mammarazzi was an endpoint to the photographer's romance. Although everything had been pure bliss in the beginning, the passing months had pointed out that they were not compatible to each other. Contacts and shared intimate moments thinned out, until they went out altogether.

The assistant driver's seat was free again — there was not

even a mirage of Mammarazzi left. Something still remained. Papparazzi had thrown on the adjacent seat a card Elisa had slipped into his jacket pocket in the vortex of the opening; in it a wistful woman was picking petals of the flowers. She had written in it the words that tore deep down in the bottom of his heart: "Pictures aren't enough."

CLOSE-UP ON FINLAND'S YOUNGEST FATHER

The reporter of *Evening News* Minna Keto rang the doorbell of an end apartment of a dingy terraced house in Jakomäki. Papparazzi let her in.

"Hi! I got here just before you. I was taking my shoes off."

In the living room they saw baby-faced Max and a more mature looking girl, Beata. They asked the newcomers to lower their voices, since their baby Daisy was sleeping in the bedroom. The writer thought that was for the best. Now they could go through the complete story of 13-year-old Max, his two years senior girlfriend Beata and their little bundle.

The *Evening News* had got an exclusive to interview the young couple at his parents' house. Beata got pregnant about a year ago and had decided to keep the baby instead of having an abortion. Having come to that conclusion meant that Max ended up becoming the youngest dad in Finland.

Max explained that they had dated only a couple of months before her pregnancy.

"I am her first boyfriend. Therefore, I am the father of Daisy."

The lassie nodded to him, being over the moon. Max had every intention of playing a close part in caring for his daughter.

"We have good and bad days, but Daisy is wonderful."

Minna steamed up.

"Okay, Max. Do you love Beata?"

"I am not quite sure… Probably!"

"Did you know how babies are made before you did it with Beata?"

"Of course, I did. We have talked about it at school. My parents have also told me about the flowers and the bees and storks."

"How is changing nappies?"

"That is Beata's job. I have tried once or twice, but the smell of that brown slurry is too much for me."

"Do you like school?"

"Not so much. It's boring. I do hate maths."

He had planned to go straight to work after comprehensive school, so he could be the best possible daddy in the whole world to his bunch. The new parents were concerned about their economics, but they had full confidence that their parents would support them. Getting the child allowance gave a security guarantee of its own.

They heard a baby starting to cry in the bedroom. In a moment Max's mother Virpi emerged from the bedroom with the baby in her arms. The little snuffles nailed everybody's attention. Virpi went to the kitchen to heat the bottle, since no breastfeeding photos were allowed. Papparazzi started pressing his button. First, he took a family photo. Max held the baby on the side of his right arm. Beata had difficulties keeping a straight face due to Minna's revolver-style questioning. It became clear that the youngsters had had sex only once around the time that the baby had been conceived.

"So, you hit the target with the first shot," Papparazzi uttered.

"Yes. I lost my virginity in a most memorable manner."

Minna asked in a straightforward way whether Beata had slept together with any other boys or men at the time. She shook her head. They had heard other kinds of versions — those indicating that Beata had been promiscuous with several partners.

"I don't care about malicious gossip! I have been true to Max."

Daisy's father and mother were so convinced of the fact that they wouldn't take a DNA test.

Minna asked if they knew of the contraceptive.

"We were not brought up in a barrel."

Max confessed that he couldn't have bought condoms before his first time. He would get cold feet.

"I wouldn't have been seeing the expression on the cashier lady's face. It could have been a too mind-blowing and flushing experience."

Virpi admitted that it was a real shock hearing about the baby.

"More so, since our son looks significantly younger than his years — just a kid himself. Almost as cuddly as Daisy."

The photographer snapped photos of Max feeding the baby in his arms. Her mouth groped the bottle greedily. The brown-haired schoolboy looked at the camera with big innocent eyes. This picture would rise to be the most viewed and clicked by far. The photo of Max kissing Daisy was a great success too.

Papparazzi and Minna thanked them for the interview. They both knew that they had a real scoop on their hands. The story was burning hot; they couldn't get soon enough to write, choose pictures and edit them. At the front door they heard

Max throwing some obstacle on the floor. Virpi lectured to her son holding her hands on her hips — just like the wives in slapstick films.

"Why did you do that? Stop it right now and learn to behave!"

Max — the fresh father who had a heavy duty of his newborn daughter for the rest of his life — climbed to his mother's lap, wept and asked for a hug.

JUST A SNEAK PEEK

Music kicked in and spotlights gleamed in Theatre Hope over a built-in catwalk. Fashion Now show had drawn in hundreds of spectators. They were seated on both sides of the catwalk. Papparazzi had placed himself in the close proximity of the elevated platform. Merle Savi, an Estonian show business multitasker, had asked or rather insisted him to come to industrial premises based in Hermanni. Merle had promised the evening would end in a Big Bang. She told Papparazzi that if he failed to come there, he would regret for the rest of his life not capturing the big buzz. For the camera dude the offer was so tempting that he couldn't refuse.

The starlet had been in the national limelight with a bang after marrying Industrial Councillor Viktor Kuusisto. The stormy relationship had ended up in a divorce a couple of years back. Merle had posed in *Playboy*, been an editor in chief for two Estonian tabloids and took part in *Big Brother Finland* and *Dancing with The Stars Finland*. Appearance was her priority, since it was a woman's worth. She had evaluated Finnish women to be inelegant matronly creatures. It was obvious that after these statements her Finnish fellow sisters had a standoffish attitude towards her.

The models walked graciously on the catwalk. The theme of the show was metamorphosis — a butterfly hatching from its cocoon. The first ladies were dressed in white hooded cloaks showing only one arm. Just barely visible. Fancy high heels clopped. Burka-style outfits passed by. The music genre changed abruptly. The pace of the overture of Giacomo Puccini's *Madama Butterfly* accelerated peacock butterflies to shining footlights. Bare heads, laid-back, loose-fitting garments, crimped skirts, vibrant neon colours, flirting with complementary colours and tops with gleaming metal rings. Papparazzi did not shoot them, but he focused his camera and searched good angles for shooting in the view of the showtime.

An expectant mood thickened in the audience until Skyfall by Adele blasted their eardrums and heavenly lights so bright that they revealed even the smallest mouse holes. Merle swooped forth in her metal-coloured dress. The slit of the dress was so high that it reached her belly button. Papparazzi's eyeballs almost popped out of their sockets once he realized that the Estonian was not having her knickers on. His keystrokes were sweaty, firing like a machine gun.

His aim was directed constantly in her groin. Mr Suits in the front row gulped down Nitros and pressed his chest; somebody called a doctor to help him. Snap, snap! Merle stole the whole show with her ballsy move. She stopped at the end of the catwalk to pose and model her outfit. Under her spread arms magically emerged butterfly wings. What a showstopper! The audience rewarded her greatest flutter of all time with loud applause.

At the VIP dinner after the show Merle revealed that she had a hidden motive for inviting Papparazzi to the show. Visual artist Karolus Aho had painted her nude. They have also developed a romantic affair. Karolus working in his Punavuori residence was a gluttonous sex machine. They made love one or three times a day. Only on those days when his agony of creating grew intolerable, their lovemaking was on hold altogether. As it turned out Karolus wanted to paint the pictures Papparazzi had taken in the show. Having an expo in Galleria Papparazzi would be a dream come true to the swinger of the brush. Papparazzi fell in love with the idea. He trusted that Mandi would warm to the idea. Merle's exhibition would be fascinatingly different from those featured so far. They shook hands on the deal. Merle — if possible — became more liberated. Blood compressed in her cheekbones and her fingers fiddled with her curls.

Can you guess what I am wearing under my skirt? Or is there anything?

This puzzle Papparazzi was going to solve that riddle that same night — that much of a playboy he was too.

MULTIPLE SHADES OF ROSEMARY

Papparazzi scanned his waterstained notebook entries sitting in his car parked on the side of the street. All the puzzle pieces were coming together. He had followed popstar Rosemary and music producer Hanski Suvanto for weeks. Rosemary was famous for her hits Katie, Crocodile Tear and The Ruler of Savanna. Their lyrics were witty and heartfelt. At the same time, they went from superficial to penetrating. The melodies were so catching that they dug into ears as earworms. Rosemary's hair colour varied from pink to red and from brown to orange with multiple shades but her eyes remained cornflower blue. In Papparazzi's mind there was no wonder that Hanski was enchanted with those petals. Rosemary had an immaculate image. She was gentle and breezy, good as an angel. One of those going to heaven. Had she forgotten that naughty girls can go anywhere they wanted?

His surveillance had started after his friend from high school days Tuomo Kivistö had revealed in a drunken blur the location of Rosemary's and Hanski's studio in Helsinki. Tuomo had regretted his bold tongue later on. Papparazzi reassured him that the info fell under source protection. The situation was volatile since Tuomo worked as building manager. The star couple worked in one of the buildings the company he worked for was managing.

The cameraman saw the lovebirds leaving the building walking arm in arm. He stepped out of his vehicle, put on coveralls and grabbed his toolkit. Tuomo had given the master key to Papparazzi to be used in gaining access to the studio. He had sworn in that even a paperclip should not go missing during the repairman's visit. If something of that kind happened or anyone was to find out about this secretive visit, he would lose his job.

In the studio Papparazzi met abruptly Sten Hammarberg who was on his way out. The atelier critic had stayed put in order to hone lyrics of the new songs. The coverall dude told him that he was going to go through the lighting and security systems and fix all the faults he detected.

The room was a complete workshop. There were loudspeakers, microphones, music stands, headphones and all kinds of miscellaneous odds and ends all over the place. On the tables there were swaying stacks of paper and the walls were decorated with gold, platinum and diamond records. There was also a recreation nook with a bar for refreshing their melody pen. On the other end of the oblong office room there was a pearly grey effect wall with an inner door. After a closer look he realized it was soundproofed. Stenkka had no idea what was behind that door. Only Hanski and Rosemary had access there. The wordsmith thought it understandable that the couple wanted some privacy. The studio was a favoured meeting place of bohemians, so there was a lot of buzz going on.

The service dude started pressing light switches and eyeing the lamps. Stenkka straightened his outerwear in the doorway.

"Bye, bye! Hopefully this won't take you too long!"

Papparazzi waved goodbye with his hand. After being left alone he started to examine the door on the effect wall once again. Pictures of the work room wouldn't bring food on the table. That's why the secret cave tempted him as a jar of honey in *Winnie the Pooh*. The master key was useless opening it. Good suggestions were vital now. In a minute he got the idea. The key to the backroom might as well be hidden somewhere on the premises. It was not found in usual places. Next, he ransacked the bar counter inside out. The key was nowhere to be found. The very last glance on the service side hit a fire column with a wine bottle stuck in the middle of it. He lifted the maul. The key with a heart-shaped keyring emerged underneath. Eureka! He held the key in his hand going to the door; it opened nicely. The scent of wood and leather flooded in his nostrils. The lighting was ambient. The walls and ceiling were painted reddish, the floor was dark wood. On the ceiling — above an octopus bed — there was hanging a steel grill; handcuffs, shiny hoops, chains, ropes and adhesive tape were hanging from it. Whips curled on the surrounding walls. Gags, masks, eye masks and clips had been arranged in their own places. On the apothecary chest of drawers by the door stood a stick rack. In addition to all the furniture was an artfully sculpted table with stools. There was another door in the love cave leading to the bathroom. It was just like any other bathroom. He picked the camera out of the toolkit and started shooting the love nest with devotion. He stayed longest at the bedside. The mattress was hard as a rock and covered with leather; satin pillows were layered by the headboard. When the tummy of the camera was full, there was time to think of all the activities happening in this room. He could see in his mind nakedness, tenderness, bondage games, cracking whips and hits on the buttocks. Pain, lust, cries and moans. Lord and dominatrix. Confidentiality agreements and safe words. He pondered what impact the soon to be published pictures in tabloids would cause on Rosemary. The conclusion was obvious: her picture — perfect image — would be torn apart for good.

Papparazzi heard somebody entering the hall. His heart jumped to his throat and his heels were on fire. He stashed the camera back in his toolkit and strode out of the sadomasochistic sanctuary closing the door behind him. Stenkka was reaching out to the hat rack.

"Fancy seeing you still here. I forgot my hat and came to collect it. Wait a second... That back room is off limits!"

Papparazzi slipped the key he had found secretly in an empty coffee mug standing on the counter and leaned on the structure.

"I just had a sneak peek, and saw that everything was okay."

"What was in there?"

"Well-equipped bedroom, where you can relax after a hard day's work."

"That's what I've been thinking all the time. What else could it be anyway?"

"Nothing else..."

They left together. They departed at the ground floor door wishing good night to each other. The labourer breathed more lightly after accomplishing his task.

WEED AND FURIOUS

Best national movies and their makers were awarded in Cable Factory. Live TV broadcasting from Jussi Gala had ended hours ago. Papparazzi was on the pursuit near the smoking spot. Taxis were coming and going. Everybody had been enjoying booze and felt that some action could be expected. The chain smokers had been photographed several times. The shutter of the camera had been flapping last, when the winner of Best Leading Lady Jussi Viola Oinonen came out to have a ciggy. Everybody wanted to talk to and congratulate her. Rapper Benito and his *Playboy* model sweetheart Charlene were also a captivating sight when they came out to get some fresh air. The lady had one of the most giving cleavages of the evening. Papparazzi had been allowed to shoot the couple but their manager had stopped him asking any questions. That was real flair.

  The tall and thin offspring of a famous acting family Kalle Korhonen and hitmaker and a man who sold his soul to the music business Artturi Alho had withdrawn themselves into a quiet corner behind the smoking spot. They were in a good spot for having their photos taken. The troll-haired music man fished from his pocket a case where he took out a hand-rolled joint. After the first burst the stick went around from mouth to mouth. They both had sturdy puffs and caught a sight first of each other and then up in the air. Actresses Kaisla Iittala and

Jutta Rautavaara joined them. The burning roll started to make bigger circles. The damsels inhaled voluptuous puffs. The discussion was carefree.

Papparazzi took his first shots without a flash but in the end, he had to put it to use. Flashing the light, he focused mostly on Kalle who puffed hard. Finally, he threw his butt towards Papparazzi.

"Suck it, bushmaster!"

The foursome got back in laughing. Papparazzi picked the butt up. The smell was distinctive — the party had smoked cannabis. Sweet aroma stuck into Papparazzi's hands. He bagged the butt as evidence.

Papparazzi jumped on the driver's seat in his car parked in a good spot. He was tired and cold. Out of the corner of his eye he watched the buzz around him. Only unimportant people around. It was always possible that some popinjay might have not been apprehended, but he couldn't help it. The clock was ticking slowly.

Papparazzi sat up when Kalle showed up holding Jussi statue in his hands. The blonde started to snap secret photos behind the window. The star got furious, dashed with Jussi pointing forward towards Kia and almost right away shattered the side window. He also banged the side of the car with the statue. In this life-threatening situation Papparazzi had no alternative but to throw the blinker on and step on it. Kalle dodged so lightsomely that he had it in him to play stunt roles as well. Yet he struck the back of the car with his fist.

On the way home his vehicle was well ventilated. Papparazzi would be throwing high fives next week when *The Week* was going to be published. It would sell out.

KARAOKE OF HORROR AT BOOK FAIR

The pressure in front of the stage at Helsinki Book Fair was intolerable. One of the sardines in a tin was Papparazzi. Singer Juhani Rahvas had just published his *The Trails Of My Life* autobiography. His most memorably hit songs were Popping Pa Hutter, Autumn Child, Blue and White Heart and The Pace of The Love. The author of the book Vesa Lehto interviewed the artist whose salt and pepper hair showed his age written in higher digits. The book had attracted commendable public attraction. Straight talk about sex had made headlines blow up. Juhani had stopped counting his flings at one hundred.

"I just read from some women's magazine that former teacher and a patch of colour Jukka Kilpinen has done the same at one thousand. Somebody always does it better!"

The author asked if it was true that at a younger age, he pushed a pine cone inside his fly to paint a picture before his photo for publication was taken.

"Let's just grant that fact to all now."

Smiles gleamed.

The easygoing conversation went on to more sincere prattle. His beaten tracks had been more of trying than carefree with his divorce and such. He declared himself to be a bad father. He had gone into debt during his success years. When his income declined, paying those debts had got devilishly hard. Sometimes negotiations with the bailiffs had been really tough. The poor box office sales and cancelled concert tours had taken its toll. He was a good singer, had even studied it in Sibelius Academy, unlike contemporary performers of simple music i.e. chanters. Recognition and awards passed him by — nobody had even suggested them. He had never been requested to join in *The Game Of Life* TV show. His songs were not in the radio playlists. Journalists had labelled him as a challenging person to work with. He recollected his recent anniversary gig in Finlandia House. The cultural editor of *Esari* had said horrible things about it.

"The person responsible for that story had no klowledge of my work or popular music whatsoever. This was a real flop from a mainstream newspaper. That scribble made one wonder if we were attending the same banquet."

You could hear bitterness in his voice.

All of a sudden, he rose from his chair, spread his legs apart, cleared his throat and started to sing. Papparazzi, lifting his camera, constantly recognized the song being one of the artist's recent production. He couldn't recall the title, but the words had soul in them.

"When you see the end of a long journey and lines on your forehead remind you of lived life. When sorrows maul and your heart freezes, only love can melt it. We all leave this all in a due course, but we all make a mark to others, remaining long. Therefore, touch gently, don't cause bruises."

The listening audience was uneasy. It had a karaoke of horrors atmosphere. The voice of the singer was hoarse and the mike cracked and screeched. The listeners voted with their feet, that is, redirected themselves. The artist flipped.

"I am sick and tired of you wax ears!"

He turned his back on the small audience and started correcting the author. The author had messed up the whole function. The penman made his conclusion and sneaked away.

Juhani said that he was going to sing another song called Cactus, the lyrics telling about how you had to hide your vulnerability under a prickly bark. There was no time for it because the staff of the fair aborted his performance and escorted him off the stage — all the way outside. The troublemaker was notified of the fact that he was not welcomed in Helsinki Fair Centre ever again.

NO PICTURES!

A hand covering a face is commonly understood sign language. A sign that the target does not want their picture taken. It is also a coveted score in the world of paparazzi — many of the top photographers use it as a motif on their book covers. Lifting a hand on your face means that you have been caught with your pants down. Therefore, lifting your hand is the most natural thing to do. Sunglasses, scarves and anything usable to cover your face indicated that you were expecting a paparazzo lurking on your heels.

Papparazzi had run into these spontaneous defensive reflexes frequently. So often that he had decided to do a No Pictures! show on the subject in his gallery with Mandi's assistance. Right before the opening night the reporter of *Yelp* Miisa Kiviaho and photographer Hilkka Alaja explored it. Papparazzi had promised a presentation of a few selected pieces of dozens of jobs to the power couple of the women's magazine. The unconditional name of the game was that he was not allowed to touch his camera at all. Hilkka took care of taking photos.

Right from the door the gaze stuck on the only large photo on the partition, in that the deceased people's artist Vinski Lehtonen peeked behind his fingers like a deer in headlights. Papparazzi told that he took the picture in the past decade in Oulu. He had heard from a most reliable source that Vinski was about to have dinner at restaurant Virta. That's where — to Lasaretti — he was going! He had waited for an hour outdoors, standing out in the wind and snow before he saw a cab pulling in front of the main entrance and the notorious four-eyes crawl out of it. He had to act quickly. The photo in the expo was taken in a way that the cab was not on the scene. The singer and songwriter had a stern expression on his face.

"Vinski told me to fuck off the whole ten seconds I had time to take his pictures. I cannot recall the exact words but they were mostly profanities. I was not allowed to enter the premises while he was dining there; he took really good care of that."

Miisa had done one-on-one interviews with him, so she had been there herself.

Vinski wasn't indeed the easiest of cases. He blurted spiteful comments. His humour was tinged with nostalgia and heavy heartedness. Irony. It was difficult for a listener to tell if one should laugh or weep when he cultivated it.

Hilkka asked Papparazzi to place himself next to the podium. She barked orders, went around and around him like a hornet.

"I never realized how difficult it could be in front of the camera!"

"Now you know how Vinski must have felt like!"

The actor and musician Juha-Matias Renko was a very challenging person to face. Later in life he had got even worse. He wanted to deal with only some of the trusted reporters and photographers by appointment only duly on time. When surprised he threw a fit. His bodyguard intervened in the proceedings with a heavy hand. Papparazzi, if anyone knew it. In his personal archives there were only overstrung photos of

Juha-Matias. Mandi had screened one of those for the exhibition. In the picture Juha-Matias angrily waved the cane he needed after diabetes damaged his legs. He was holding a box of fast food.

"This was taken in Macca's on Teollisuuskatu. I had just finished my cheeseburger when I saw Juha-Matias was walking laboriously inside. I fetched my camera from the car and stayed put waiting for his exit. He emerged quite shortly in front of my lens. Can you guess what he shouted at me?"

"No pictures!"

"Exactly. I took them anyway — in spite of everything."

In front of the exhibition photo Papparazzi contemplated why Juha-Matias had always taken such a distrustful and venomous attitude towards him. He was still baffled by it. Probably he would never find out.

The trio shifted to the smallest picture of the expo. A musician Joakim Mustonen, who presently made "a living out of TV work, pointed his fingers at the camera, his gaze turned aside. Papparazzi had taken it years ago.

The reporter of *Smirk* was interviewing Joakim in Kiasma Café. Her first question was about his past as a gospel artist. That was too much to him and he got on her back for talking about it. When the second question came out in a fumble, he accused her of being poorly prepared.

The photo shooting was the last straw.

"I snapped four or five frames. His mitt covered his face in all of them. I became frustrated and took a hike in the middle of it. None of the shots were ever published — on Joakim's demand. The magazine illustrated the story with his promotional material."

Bloke Out of Order, the assembly's blood curdling sized

horizontal picture from Tavastia aroused admiration in Hilkka and Miisa.

"I went there well before the band's gig. To my surprise they were all five of them hanging out in the parlour. I started shooting off. As you can see most of them covered their faces with their hand. Only the guitar player Rontte did something different, that is, giving me a finger."

"The outcome is gorgeous! Much better than a normal pose picture."

"I couldn't agree more. Let's just empathize that they were just fooling around in that situation. There was no negative aspect in it."

Many of the household names enjoyed their dinner frequently in Restaurant Nokka that resided in Kanavaranta. Miisa and Hilkka watched astonished at a picture where the waiter was hitting Papparazzi on the head with a dustbin lid in front of Nokka. Behind them they could see a ship's propeller and an anchor mounted in the brick wall, fitting well on the intimidating atmosphere of the photo.

"What's happening here?"

"A couple of years back I was on the watch at dusk in front of Nokka to see which celebs entered and exited the restaurant. As it happened there were so many of them that they were knocking each other out. Noel Arkila and Janna Kuusi, Mikko Leppijärvi and Miss Ada and many others. The waiter got a grasp of me, took something to fight with and bolted out."

"What did he shout at you?"

"Take a hike, you scoundrel, stop harassing our customers! Get lost, orc! Something like that. He missed my head but it was a close call. This Fury picture has now its premiere here."

The *Yelp* duo noticed a photo of former Prime Minister Toivo Piipponen's spouse Johanna who was walking on Dagmarinkatu carrying a bag of groceries. She was holding her other hand on top of her cheek and ear. That way she tried to protect herself from Papparazzi's attack. She was looking down.

"Johanna is always so elegant — except in this picture. Her hair is a mess, maybe even unwashed for several days, no makeup, she is wearing a worn out cardigan, sweatpants and slippers given as a present from her grandmother. This photo is one of my first ambushes in Helsinki, I drove back and forth between the Parliament House and Etu-Töölö. I did get some shots of Johanna in Café Marocco, but this one of the bag lady was a more suitable pick for this exhibition," Papparazzi said.

"Her whole essence is screaming: don't take any pictures," Miisa commented.

"That's why it is so good and authentic," Hilkka stated.

Last but not least they were staring at the Five-Spice Girls showing the finger to Papparazzi from the back seat of a taxi. Aino and Taina Savolainen laughed out loud while doing it. Taina's other hand was in no pictures position.

"They were partying in Milliklubi the week before last. I stormed to shoot them at that point when they were leaving the premises feeling a bit tipsy. We were counting the small hours — if we were up to do it. They had fixed a friend to pick them up from Kaivokatu."

Mandi joined in with Papparazzi, Miisa and Hilkka.

"These kinds of pictures are quite typical in the world of paparazzi. In a car the stars are tight as bees in a hive — they have got nowhere to go. A competent photographer can have a field day on those occasions."

"Unless the car windows are tinted," Papparazzi stated.

At the end of their round the foursome drank coffee from paper cups in the natural light colouring them flooding through the shop windows. Mandi showed the Yelpians her desk by the front door and the sales outlet connected to it. Field literature and other prop-like scarves Papparazzi had made famous were on sale. Especially Hilkka examined the supply with interest. The itch in Papparazzi's hands grew up to the point that he grabbed his beloved tool. Oh yeah! The subjects covered their faces…

THE ULTIMATE PUKKI PARTY FEAT SANTA

Papparazzi, Nella and Eeli were following the ignition of the Christmas lights in Aleksanterinkatu. The event was one of the highlights of the year. It brought Christmas into people's hearts. Santa's and the Mayor Jan Vapaavuori's arrival at Senaatintori riding a Jumbo antique tram brought a star twinkle in children's eyes.

Grandpa Gang was able to greet Santa up close. Red suits handed out surprise coupons to children and Eeli and Nella were part of that lucky group. The gang plunged to study what was on it. "You are welcome to Café Engel after the Christmas Parade! You are allowed to enter the premises by showing this coupon at the door. The elves will serve Christmassy snacks and beverages. There are also some happy little surprises waiting for you! Yours Santa."

Although the invitation stretched their schedule tremendously, they went to the café anyway. Christmassy decorations were set out with good taste. The gang was directed to their table near the window by the elves. In under an hour the whole room was full of children, their parents and grandparents and above all a joyful expectant atmosphere. The suspense was palpable. What is it about? That was what everyone wanted to know. Papparazzi was not going to be surprised empty handed, on the contrary he was going to catch all the interesting stuff inside his camera. That was something he had already accomplished.

Gingerbread, mince pies and hot beverages were served on their dark wooden table. They grabbed the goodies. The flavours hugged the stomach. The elves regrouped around the display case and sang some of the most popular Christmas carols so that the walls crumbled. Songs culminated into Santa Claus is Coming to Town, with The Master of Korvatunturi entering the premises carrying a large sack on his shoulder. More and more sacks were brought in — soon there was a big pile. Kids' eyes grew even brighter. Gifts!

"Are there any kind children around here?"

"Yes!"

The white bearded old grandpa beckoned to the same door he had just entered himself. One of the elves started to beat the drum.

"I welcome here my prestigious helper... Teemu Pukki!"

They saw the iconic leading goalscorer of Finland's National Football Team aka Eagle Owls and Norwich City. He was wearing the same jersey with number ten on the back he used playing for the Owls. On his head he was wearing a Christmas hat. Applause and cries of joy continued indefinitely.

The duo revealed the nature of the event.

"Since Finland qualified for the top football tournament for the first time ever, the European Championships, we decided to combine our forces and arrange The Ultimate Pukki Party featuring Santa," Father Christmas announced.

"So, we are also making history at the moment! Every child in here gets a football with our autographs and a jersey with number ten on the back in their own size."

"Jee! It was so worth coming here!" Nella and Eeli glowed.

The elves scattered around with their sacks and helped the children get right-sized jerseys. The sacks emptied quickly. Santa and Teemu Pukki sat on the longest table and gave their pen hands a hard time.

When the Grandpa Gang's turn was on, Nella and Eeli missed one or two heartbeats. The bearded men asked the children's names and hobbies. Both answered loud and clear and told that they were into multiple sport activities, including football.

"Good!"

"Do you believe in Father Christmas?"

"Yes, we do. Both of you!"

Teemu Pukki handed them their presents with sunny eyes. They thanked him smiling happily. Papparazzi was going on strong with his camera.

All good things must come to an end. This too. There was a media mob formed outside, both national and international. They had not been let in. The Pukki and Santa duo came out hands on each other's shoulders. The fireworks of flashlights blinded eyes. Papparazzi joined in and chuckled with content since he had taken photos from inside also. Those were the most valuable ones!

HOLIDAY PERMIT GRANTED, MISTER PRIME MINISTER

Prime Minister Petteri Sierilä was on a vacation in Corfu with his wife Hilla-Maarit. *The Week* had found out and they had alerted Papparazzi to go after them. The magazine paid the bill. The photographer had booked in the hotel the previous day. The Sierilä couple enjoyed their holiday at the same place. Papparazzi hadn't seen them yet. He was tuning his equipment sitting in the shadow of an olive tree. The old tree was several tens of metres away from the pool area, where he expected the sweethearts' arrival. It was an early morning. The peace in the heat was broken only by the endless concert of cicadas. He had prepared himself for a long wait with his camping chair, back bag and cooler.

Papparazzi had given an impression to everybody that he was a nature photographer. At the reception he had shown pictures of birds and enthused about the shooting opportunities of this paradise island. A WWF cap, animal theme in his T-shirt and camouflage cargo shorts covered his body. He had let the beard on his chin grow, his eyes were covered with sunglasses. Binoculars were hanging on a strap on top of his chest. Mostly he just sat and read magazines. He also took some photos of the lumpy olive tree as a bluff. He gave a lecture of nature photographing to a few passers-by. Getting a top quality picture would require a bit of luck, skill and diligence again this time. Everybody wished him luck in his endeavours.

The temperature rose up to forty degrees during the day. He used a lot of sunscreen and water bottles emptied with pace. In order to avoid dehydration, furthermore he also visited the stall-style pool bar. Greek coffee without sugar kept him alert. Medium sweet sparkling wine on the rocks had become his favourite. He was served by pineapple-style-haired Andreas, with whom he had hit it off right away, so Papparazzi decided to come clean on his real reason for coming to Gouvia. He showed him pictures of the Finnish Prime Minister and his wife. Andreas promised to blab everything he saw and heard about the couple in order to get big tips. Since he was the one to consecrate a secret he promised that he would not breathe it to another living soul. Papparazzi returned to his base to nod off.

Just a second! There the lovedoves were coming to the pool surrounded by yellow deckchairs. The Prime Minister had swimming shorts by Hugo Boss as a part of his holiday attire. Hilla-Maarit was wearing a black Jasmine swimsuit. Papparrazzi stood up, stretched his legs and attached the camera on the podium. Hilla-Maarit and Petteri paid no attention to him. Kissing and caressing each other. Hilla-Maarit also pampered her hubby with a neck massage. They were fumbling with their phones. Every now and then the duo took a dive in the pool and bought drinks from Andreas. They flopped with their flipflops to the side of the pool sipping their colourful cocktails. Pictures were stored on a memory card.

The lovers bathed in the sun for several hours. Mostly they relaxed and napped in their chairs. Papparazzi followed their example as well. He dozed off in minutes. When he woke up, Petteri and Hilla-Maarit were nowhere to be seen. Andreas told him that he had created both of them drinks using his artistic freedom. He had put vodka, Aperol, red vermouth and thyme in the Prime Minister's drink. Hilla-Maarit had gulped down a drink containing Limoncello, tequila and lemon verbena. They had asked incidentally who that tree hugger carrying binoculars and camera might be. Andreas had convinced them that he was a harmless twit. The only thing that the birder was interested in were the birds spinning in the air. They had sighed in relief — a paparazzo would have been something that they had dreaded. They had made an arrangement with their bodyguard that they could get some one-on-one time for making out on the holiday. He had stayed indoors watching TV. Papparazzi ordered a frosted glass of beer and greased it profusely. After emptying his pint of beer, he went back to the tree and packed up. It was time to retire back to his room to contemplate his next move.

 Dressed in well-groomed attire the Prime Minister with his spouse enjoyed their dinner in La' Kantas tavern, where they served traditional Greek dishes and drinks. Seafood was their speciality. The lovedoves sat on an open well-lit patio. Papparazzi had hidden himself in the shadows of dusk to find the best angle for shooting. There would be no need to use flashlight. When stretching his ears, he could hear their light conversation. Once in a while the main street was so crowded that his auditory condition was disturbed. The camera hero snapped pictures while their pre-meal drinks and appetizers were served on the table. Suddenly the Prime Minister lifted his hand and snapped his fingers. A muscular guy wearing a short-sleeved shirt started off to the shooter. Papparazzi immediately recognized him being the bodyguard.

"Nature photographer doing his job?"

Papparazzi felt a loss of words. He had to make something up and do it asap.

"This is it! When you look around with open eyes, people in this tourist trap are part of the nature —more than anything."

"So, your busy work has nothing to do with having a Prime Minister dining with his spouse just across the street?"

"I have noted the fact. There's no way denying it."

"I don't think you will deny the fact that they are the only people you have been photographing."

Papparazzi tried to work around it but in the end, he had actually been revealed earlier on by using search the fucking Google method.

"You made the Prime Minister suspicious — something in your character raised some issues. The pool area of a hotel is not the most usual habitat where a nature photographer lurks. Although you had disguised yourself as being one quite inventively, it wasn't that hard to spot you on the Internet as yourself and as being really you — Papparazzi."

The security man asked next in which magazine the shots were going to end up. He rushed to forward the message to the Sieriläs and came back short of breath.

"They are very understanding for you. You can go and have a chat with them."

Papparazzi did as he was told. When introducing himself to the couple he took off a bit of his disguise by taking off his cap and shoving it into his camera bag.

"You do understand that we could raise quite a commotion at will," Hilla-Maarit started.

"Since we've had a few hours to digest this and the first emotional turmoils have calmed down, we can let slip everything that has happened so far if your activities end here and now," Petteri continued.

It was OK to Papparazzi. Come to think of it, he had lots of pictures of the duo as it was. The atmosphere became relaxed right away. The couple asked him to join in. He was served a glass of ouzo diluted with soda water. Hilla-Maarit was anxious to know how the photos had succeeded.

"You are not going to put forward any dubious material, are you?"

"There is nothing improper in this! We're a married couple, who cares if we kissed so that everybody can see it?"

Papparazzi admitted that the Prime Minister had hit the target.

"The case would be totally different if one of you were enjoying yourselves with a secret lover."

"As if we would! There is nothing odd going on!"

It was more difficult for Hilla-Maarit to bear being seen in her swimsuit.

"You cannot publish any photos showing my belly sausages."

Papparazzi promised to choose pictures with a good taste. While anise spirit warmed his tummy pleasantly it was time to make his departure. While he was pushing uphill on the road to Paradise Hotel in the heat of the night, he came to a conclusion that this play of dressing up could have ended in a worse disaster. This was the final proof of the fact that the publicity did win the heat every time.

The entertainment magazine asked Papparazzi to finalize the whole affair by meeting the couple in Helsinki-Vantaa airport when they returned on a straight flight from Corfu after their holiday. Their return interested also other media representatives. Hilla-Maarit and Petteri arrived at the arrival lobby of Terminal Two tanned and relaxed. The security personnel followed on their heels. The Prime Minister told them that they had a nice and romantic holiday.

After the biggest buzz was over Papparazzi received a text message. "I wish that the Parliament's next Question Time would make as big headlines as our vacationing. Thanks for the pictures anyway! Regards from P.S. P.S: Andreas told us everything."

RED-EYE FLIGHT ON A FAST TRACK

Papparazzi tore himself from his everyday hard labour to a vacation. The red-eye flight from Helsinki to Peking on Finnair's business class was a new experience for him. The Great Wall and Tiananmen Square were the places to see for him. Peaceful music playing on from the speaker unit, champagne sparkling in a glass. The seat beside the window was comfortable and it could be laid flat for sleeping. The seats were arranged diagonally in a herringbone pattern, which added to travel convenience.

Take off was only minutes away. Members of the cabin crew were having a subdued conversation in a way suggesting that something extraordinary was about to happen. It didn't take long to speculate it. A Formula One star Niko Saarinen and his spouse Sointu sailed in wearing luxury garments. The couple was guided into their seats on his right. They had adjacent centre seats. A wave of frustration struck in his consciousness immediately — he had packed his camera bag inside his suitcase placed in the cargo hold. He should have taken at least his camera in his hand luggage! There was nothing he could do about it now. The smartphone was the only shooting equipment available. He could remember well the world famous Don Cale's remorse on not taking pictures of Marilyn Monroe in the beginning of his career. He never got a second chance. The teaching of the lesson was that when the bright Venus is shining in front of you, always grab your camera. Niko and Sointu were two of the most famous faces in our country and ambassadors abroad. These photos had to be taken, but not just yet. It was going to be an eight-hour flight so he could take his time to wait for the right moment. The captain announced that they were ready for take off. It was swift and controlled. The soundproofing was so effective that the sound of the engines was almost inaudible.

It was dinnertime. Papparazzi ate crabs, duck rillettes, trout, corn purée and ice cream. And of course, there was also an ample selection of beverages to go with the meal. Out of the corner of his eye he could see that Niko and Sointu were drinking like a fish. They were burbling in a buzz. Eating dessert made no difference. On the contrary since Niko started singing: "Little cognac is going down, going down, going down…"

The steward encouraged the warbler and brought him some more joy water to drink. There were a lot of cabin crew members buzzing around the household names. Some of them even gave them hugs. Sointu chatted with some so friendly that Papparazzi realized that they had a history of working together. The brunette beauty used to work as a stewardess. Presently she was a corporate wife running businesses of her own.

The atmosphere calmed down after three or four hours of the flight when the cabin crew started having their breaks and more and more of the passengers cuddled up under their soft blankets to catch some sleep. Papparazzi noticed how Sointu moved nearer to Niko snapping into his lap. The hand of the F1 champion slid on Sointu's bosom. Giggles and snogging.

The time of action was on. The blond-curly-header rose up, because there was a low piece of the wall blocking his view to the seat of the Formula One star. He started to snap photos without the flash. After about ten snaps he viewed his loot with a sugary face. Two or three of them were right on target — both Niko's hands were holding Sointu's pulleys as keen as he had held the steering wheel when he was competing. Sointu caressed Niko's crotch. There was something hard, but at the same time something soft and tender. Papparazzi made a conclusion out of their whispering that they were going to do something they had contemplated many times before: to join in the Mile High Club. They slipped to the toilet in the middle section of the cabin. Papparazzi pussyfooted after them and pushed his ear to the door. Behind it he could hear sensuous moaning.

The stalker sat on the nearest available seat and got himself into a posing position as if he was going to take selfies. In actuality his focus was on the place where the Saarinen couple were indulging their lovemaking. After five minutes the door opened. The vigilant watchdog of the fourth estate captured the way the duo emerged out of it one after another. They were still so excited with each other that they did not pay attention to anything else around them. Their steps were hastened with a strong feeling that they hadn't been caught after their trick.

Papparazzi took his turn locking himself in the toilet. It was open and well lit. There was also a window and a plant in a jar. He took his time to take plenty of shots, returning to his seat. They made a sensational ensemble he could sell as soon as he landed to be published transnationally. Remake the front pages and issues.

A SUMMIT MEETING WITH MR BEAVER

The filming of a new TV series *Those Were The Days* featuring a character loved by people, Mr Beaver, was on in Rööperi. The media had a chance to follow it from Iso Roobertinkatu. Papparazzi was also on the spot. Mr Beaver was best known for his slogan: Yes, this made my bile boiling!

The old grumpy bastard had difficulties in adapting to the trends of modern world. His opinions were firm and unchanged through times. From the character it was easy to find features of your father, grandfather or grumbling neighbour.

The actor Kimmo Heikkinen playing the part of Mr Beaver wanted to get some time alone. The fuss made his head spin. He strutted in his costume around the corner, where Papparazzi had sneaked to for the same reason. They maintained a polite distance. An old lady emerged out of the blue pushing a rollator; she greeted the actor cheerfully making him confused. What would be the right way to react? The professional made a spontaneous decision.

"The sun glare is so hot that it makes my bile boiling!"

Papparazzi rose to the occasion immediately and started off with his camera. Nobody had any idea what the outcome of this summit meeting would be.

The old lady had a gentle smile on her face before she got

serious. As if she had deliberated the comment she had just heard once more and recognized its controversy.

"Are you feeling all right?"

A meaningful silence followed her comment. The actor had to dig deep into his brains when pondering the right answer.

"Things could be better. I haven't had my portion of brown gravy and potatoes. They are offering me crickets, but yes, it is not all right by me."

"If you come with me, I will cook you a proper meal."

Mr Beaver declined the offer politely. There was no chance for him to disengage from the filming for a such a long period of time.

"Can I ask you what are you doing in the big city?"

"Yes, I came to Helsinki to share my teaching and correct misconceptions. The music is broken. The athletes sit their asses down. Saunas go down unused. Where is this country going? I'm just asking."

The granny wished from the bottom of her heart that the farmer fella could get his doctrine to hit home. Her rationalization was evident.

"Everything was better in the past."

"Those were the days!"

The silver fox waved her hand as goodbye and started off again. Both Papparazzi and Mr Beaver got water in their eyes. They were lost for words to tell why they were weeping. You needed pictures for that — and they were fortunate to have had them of the unforgettable summit meeting.

FOOLING AROUND WITH ACQUAINTANCES

Papparazzi hid behind a bush of a two-storey terraced house near Vartionkylänlahti. He had spotted the sensational blonde Larissa Isotalo downtown and dashed after a Beemer she was steering in his own car. The sex bomb was one of the permanent celebs, but her real breakthrough had been when she started dating the rally superstar Jori-Teppo Santanen. Larissa had moved to the racer's gorgeous detached house in Kauhava soon after they made their romance public. Jori-Teppo travelled a lot abroad and this was not the beauty's normal place of residence. The bush shooter was fired with enthusiasm. These photos would sell like hot cakes. He was certain that the mover and shaker of crap journalism hadn't noticed her stalker. She had driven a mobile phone on her ear the whole time. She had parked her BMW in front of the entrance in an easy-going way, although it was prohibited to drive into the yard by a traffic sign. Papparazzi's car was on the side of the road.

The bushmaster got his first shots when the busty lady took garbage bags to the shed, her long blond hair waving in the wind. Tight leggings and T-shirt enhanced her sexy appearance. Black and white sneakers complemented her overall look. The scarf man photographed with so much devotion that his finger got cramp. He had enough time to get it into condition since it took hours without any other movement around the flat but the leaves in the tree.

At dusk the blonde emerged wearing jeans full of holes with a tall, broad-shouldered and dark-haired man. He smoked a cigar before he hopped into the car. This time the handsome man was driving. The status was captured on the camera. Papparazzi let the unwed couple go on their way. He was speeding home to sell his shots. Big numbers went around in his head.

Many scoops have been spoiled by scrutiny. In *Smirk* they had inspected image files Papparazzi had sent them long and hard, with a magnifying glass and contacted parties involved. Judgement was clear. Larissa was not in the pictures — it was her doppelgänger or possibly her sister. It was an easy mistake to make; they were so look-alike. Iikka Ahtola made the fatal call to the photo man who stalked in Vuosaari.

"You have been shooting nobodies! And they a) are not a bit interesting, and b) they enjoy the protection of privacy. These pictures go in to the trash."

Papparazzi did his own comparisons on his home computer. The final result was the same as the gossip magazine had. How could he have made a mistake like that? He could have sworn that he had been on the right track. He had never been so pissed off.

During that time Jimi Körkkö from *The Week* shot Larissa having a sleepover with some CT boss in Kauniainen. "Larissa's unfaithfulness has been tipped off from several sources. You must have had them. Finally, I caught the cheater red-handed. The feeling is incredible." Papparazzi read a bragging text message Jimi sent him while doing his evening routine. His feelings of joy at his colleague's success were mixed with envy.

REGAL AND FLORAL SPLENDOUR

The Bachelorette Eevi Reponen and the one holding her heart for Taneli Wallenberg had been adamant on not giving any public announcements after the ending of the latest season of *Bachelorette Finland* TV show. This annoyed all the media houses so much that some of them banned them. The *Evening News* wanted to slap these tight-lipped lovers by hiring Papparazzi to do their deed. The savage of Pikku Huopalahti had been able to tighten the loop around them but failed to get any pictures.

Currently he was taking crucial steps toward his goal in Cherry Garden of Roihuvuori where there was the Hanami event going on. He was given a tip from a person who had heard the previous week that Eevi and Taneli were going to attend to the viewing celebration of the pin flowers. Since he had plenty of time to prepare himself for the oncoming event and he wanted to surprise the duo red-handed he had disguised himself as a cosplay character. His costume improved his prospects versus having to use his own attire. He strutted towards the stage as King Sindbad. He had borrowed the costume from a passionate industry enthusiast who was about the same size as Papparazzi and had this glamorous ensemble ready and waiting. The outfit consisted of a white robe, violet harem pants, pointed red shoes and a blue shirt under the white robe. The character had long lilac hair. On his head he had a white turban decorated with feathers. His appearance was perfected with coloured contact lenses. He was carrying a metal container where he had hidden his camera. There was a scimitar hanging from his belt.

Almost everyone he met was carrying some sort of camera. They wanted to capture the sea of flowers mostly to be published in social media. Papparazzi eyed around to catch a glimpse of Eevi and Taneli. Logically a crowd of fans would be flocking around the couple. Since there were no signs of them, he decided to get some snack. There were all kinds of Japanese food sold in the stalls. Sushi was his choice of snack.

The female vendor asked whether the colourful character was one of the actors in Kyogen theatre. Papparazzi shook his head — he had never heard of it — and introduced himself as being a cosplay man. Sindbad was a well-known skirt chaser.

"Beware of getting caught in my tripwire," Papparazzi warned as he was withdrawing aside with his dish.

She was in the spirit and laughed sweetly.

The mistress of ceremonies asked the Bachelorette to join him to announce the winner of the Cherry Princess Diploma this spring. The robed man's gaze was focused when he saw the Bachelorette alive for the first time. Beside Eevi walked a crowned female introduced as Cherry Blossom Queen. The title of Princess was granted to Venla Halme, a student from Turku. Eevi and the Queen adjusted a flower-patterned kimono with a sash on Venla and put a wreath on her head. After an interview with the Queen and the Princess it was Eevi's turn. The TV star admitted she was still dating Taneli.

"Is it true that you have been drawing a tight line on the media since the TV show broadcasting ended?"

"Yes, it is! We haven't given any interviews together and shooed all the paparazzi away from the heels."

"Why are you so adamant on it?"

"The answer is genuinely Finnish. Whoever has the happiness, let them hide their happiness."

"Can you specify it more thoroughly?"

"We want our relationship to develop without distractions from outside. The media are attacking us so confrontationally these days."

The name of the game was made clear to everybody. King Sindbad had to strike immediately when Eevi and Taneli hooked up. The turban head cast his empty paper plate to the trash and pushed himself nearer the stage. An elderly lady was so pissed off with his cutting through that she hit him on the side with her parasol. He had no choice but to dive in the cloudy waters. He got there in the nick of time when Eevi walked down the stairs on the side of the stage. Taneli met the maiden at the foot of the stairs.

"Hi! I am a big fan of both of you. Can I have a word with you?"

"Of course, you can!"

It was apparent that they were living their dream. They had a lot of common features — they even laughed at the same things. They had spent hot moments the previous evening on a sauna raft and enjoyed skinny dipping. The camera came out before they knew when the hearts glared in their eyes.

"Pack your smile! I'll take wonderful pictures of you two together!"

Snap, snap!

"Wait a second! What character are you exactly?"

"I am a cosplay enthusiast. Usually people think about

teenage girls with their cream cake dresses, but most of us are grown ups."

"Who are you supposed to be?"

"An Asian king and seaman, Sindbad."

"And under that outfit hides… who?"

His answer wasn't on the spot, which raised Eevi's and Taneli's suspicions. Papparazzi tried to remove their doubts as well as he could.

"It doesn't matter. I am just a regular guy. It is nice to turn my dull everyday greyness to this festive colourfulness."

Just to make sure the lovey-doves wanted him to present his ID. He declined to do so; instead he started to snap photos from the close proximity.

"There is something wrong about all of this! This Tivoli runaway joker can be a paparazzo in disguise!"

They glanced at each other quickly, turned on their heels and bolted hand in hand.

Sindbad tried to follow them but he tripped over his own feet. He heard hands clapping around him.

"Nice comic performance! The best show today!"

Sindbad thanked them for the praises and checked that his photos had succeeded. They had. Since he hadn't taken his car with him it was time get loaded in honour of his achievement. He had to get some of the Japanese wise men's drink called sake asap.

PAPPARAZZI'S ABOMINATION

The rapper Zimo's songs were played on the radio on a regular basis and collected millions of streaming in Spotify. He had cleaned up the whole tableful of prizes in the most recent Emma Gala. He avoided publicity like it was a contagious disease but he could afford to do it. Papparazzi saw how the hotel manager received the golden-blond-haired Viking in front of Kalastajatorppa. After exchanging pleasantries, the duo went inside. The photographer hid in a nearby smoking spot. The winter night would stretch long if Zimo had booked a room from the hotel. He could end up shooting in the morning. A dinner or bar flying would be a better option — he would be able to surprise the star during the same evening or night. Although the place was sheltered the wind from the sea shook the shivering man with both hands from time to time. The fingers and toes took the first hit and then the whole body followed through. At three o'clock in the morning he was convinced that Zimo had gone to bed. Papparazzi slogged to his car, put the heater on full and drove home.

After a few hours of rest the newspaper photographer stalked again in Munkkiniemi. He had put on several layers of clothes and thermo boots. The claws of frost had to work extremely hard to get into his bones. He had decided to stay put until the breakfast time was over. Tic, toc, the clock was ticking — without anything mentionable happening. At ten he had to stamp his feet and move his arms in order to keep warm. Almost immediately Zimo emerged holding tenderly his hand on the shoulder of a dark-skinned handsome guy wearing a beanie. The artist was bisexual, so he had been spotted with both male and female companions over the years. Papparazzi was ready to bet a larger sum for the fact that this black guy was a new conquest.

When the cab whizzed in front of the main entrance the shooter got moving. The lovers spotted the unwanted Jack Frost running nearer to them holding his outstretched camera. Zimo let go of his companion lightsomely. Something looking like a hairdryer emerged in his hand starting to flash lights every time Papparazzi snapped his. The duo pushed themselves onto the back seat of the taxi while the gadget still flashed on unceasingly. The door slammed shut while the flashing went on both sides. The photographer was baffled when he watched the taillights going further away. A glimpse in his camera revealed that he hadn't managed to snap a single sharp picture of the couple.

When at home a net search revealed that Zimo had used a device protecting him from a paparazzo — in this case Papparazzi — taking pictures. The pricy gadget was for famous people who wanted to walk in peace in public places. It was marketed as a step towards a protected world with more privacy. Although Papparazzi was depressed that Zimo had pulled his leg the name of the device made him smile: Paparazzo's Abomination.

ABSOLUTELY RADISHING EXHIBITION

Mandi had allured Papparazzi to join her at the Tiipii Gallery in Urho Kekkosen katu for the opening of Saima Kahila's Green Tinges exhibition. Mandi and Saima had been old acquaintances since their student days. The newspaper photographer was going to get a guaranteed scoop with a high probability that he would be the only media representative on the spot. Although the bob-haired visual artist had notified about her oncoming opening to several media houses, none of them had been bothered to arrive. There were a lot of art lovers covering the loss.

Right after Papparazzi entered the gallery from the main entrance he was handed a glass of sparkler. On the wall on the right side was a curtain covering the magnum opus of the exhibition. It was to be revealed soon. Before that they were able to circle around all the other creations. There were mostly still lives of fruit — paintings, drawings and sculptures — with a contemporary twist. On the table there were bowls full of samples which the guests nibbled standing. Saima told Papparazzi that her pieces represented her emotions and ideas; the creative process had been manic.

"I found a witch within me when I was moulding them. In ancient times they would have burnt me at the stake."

The mundane fruit and vegetables reflected her inner world overflowing with colours — especially green.

"Formerly I sought inspiration from the outside, this time it came from my inner being. I never planned them, I created them intuitively."

Papparazzi was all ears. It was captivating to hear where Saima's art welled up. The artist pressed the photographer to enjoy the art work and the buffet turning to the guest next to her. Papparazzi associated himself with Mandi. She was also carrying her camera gear.

"What do you think?"

"Absolutely radishing exhibition!"

"The biggest bang is yet to go off, that is the thing behind that curtain."

After a quarter of an hour Saima jingled a bell while retreating to the purple hanging on the wall. The murmur of the audience toned down.

"Dear friends! The time has come to reveal the magnum opus of my exhibition. The Green Ting was such a mind-blowing experience that after I finished it, I couldn't eat, sleep or make love for a week."

The curtain was drawn and everyone gasped. There was a cucumber tied up on the wall with duct tape.

The gallerist brought more of them on a bowl for the guests to nibble. Papparazzi, Mandi and several other people grabbed their camera gear. When Saima told that she had sold the Green Ting to an art collector in Qatar for 100,000 euros it made the whole space stirring. The buyer wanted to remain anonymous. Globally these kinds of news bombs were familiar but Finland was a different story. Around these parts an artist and a starveling were one and the same.

In front of the Green Ting people were taking selfies, some of them crunching cucumbers. One of them grabbed the cucumber from the wall and took a bite of it. The girl with specs shrieked:

"The most expensive treat of my life!"

A couple of hippie-looking guys attacked the lass, grabbing the partially eaten cucumber out of her hand. A jumble followed. People were bemoaning the brutal destruction of a priceless art work. Nobody should be touching the art! Papparazzi and Mandi were up to date. Shots were fired. Saima looked as she didn't mind the commotion as she just taped a new cucumber on the wall. She clapped her hands in order to turn their attention to herself.

"Hi everybody! You just witnessed a prearranged performance connected to my magnum opus! Visual artist Linda Kiukas was the thief and gallerist Heidi Salin videotaped the performance to better reuse."

Both mentioned waved their hands with joy. The peace was restored in the gallery. Here and there people were complimenting the Green Ting speaking to the viewers on many different levels. The cucumbers symbolized the global trade. The artist had managed to turn a mundane vegetable into a source of stinging critics and humour. Some of them had tears in their eyes.

Saima made it clear to Mandi and Papparazzi while saying farewells that the buyer didn't actually make a purchase of the cucumber but did authenticate the art work. The cucumber was not supposed to be preserved indefinitely; it could be swapped periodically. The visual artist enthused that anyone could copy the work and exhibit in their own homes.

"You can get into the newest breeze just on the cost of one euro! Think about that. And do it yourself."

She gave them each a cucumber.

"I recommend that you use painter's tape instead of duct tape so you don't leave marks on the wall."

MONSTERS IN THE NIGHT

The Earl was one of the most successful pop rock groups of Finland whose members had always performed in jet-black costume masks. Other colours were flagrant and studs grossly big. On the stage the fivesome was a frightening sight. The front man of the group was Mr Earl, Jari Poutiainen. There were no published photos of him without the monster mask. The situation was different abroad; he had been presented in many tabloids without the monster mask, in covers as well. After the Swedish *Aftonbladet* took off Mr Earl's mask *The Week* decided that it was time to let the Finns see the star as himself.

Papparazzi got a moneyed assignment to strike on the heels of Mr Earl living in Tapiola, Espoo. His exact address was a mystery even in the magazine. Only one thing was known — Jari had been spotted walking his two American Bulldogs in Riistapolku. Days and nights had elapsed in the shade of pines and birches doing nothing. After he had eaten his own packed lunches and drunk coffee from a thermo mug it was time to go to Shopping Mall Ainoa to get a proper lunch. It was a risk. It was possible that at the same time Jari would be moving around close to home with his big mutts. It was not a very plausible occurrence to miss the star. He might as well be on vacation. The other alternative was that he was being a house mouse. They hadn't booked any gigs this week.

Fortune favours the bold at last. Bloke in black, up to his hood, closed up the cameraman straight in front of him. His face was fully visible. Papparazzi jumped out of his car, focused on to the target and let his instrument yodel. Although there was no chance that Jari couldn't notice the shooting he continued his calm stroll forward not turning his head away until he was just alongside. He didn't say a word walking past Papparazzi. His facial expression was tense. The dogs hit him with an irritated glare, spit gleaming on their jaws of steel. They were kept well under control by their owner, so the shooter was not threatened by them.

After the shooter lost sight of Jari and his furry friends Papparazzi went through his catch. It was excellent, including the close-ups. It was time to bid farewell to Riistapolku.

The next week's issue of *The Week* had Jari Poutiainen as its cover boy and made an unprecedented hoo-ha that flabbergasted both the magazine and the photographer. People had the right to know the true face of the celebrity without the mask on. The media had been far too nice to him protecting his Santa-like fairy tale. The Finns didn't agree with them. They thought that the magazine was guilty of blasphemy. It was boycotted, orders were canmobile phoneed and issues tampered on the stalls. Some of the malls refused to sell the issue containing the unveiling images. The feedback column filled up with filthy messages. It was Papparazzi's first time being targeted. The loudest fans of The Earl urged people to attack him on social media. He got hate mail. He stopped answering calls from unknown numbers — from the first ones churned out they had already contained something unprintable.

One night he heard his doorbell ringing. When Papparazzi

opened his door, it was torn wide open. Four monsters in their black costumes were gawking at him from the stairwell. The Earl! The foremost and the grimiest of them, Mr Earl, asked the photographer to come along with them.

"What is it about?"

"This is about those photos you took of me. The whole state has been feeling sick after they were published. It has messed up our lives, heads and kits. We need to talk with you!"

Mr Earl introduced the monsters standing behind him: Lucas, electric guitarist, Ramen, bass player, and Pööpi, drummer. Everybody nodded when their name was mentioned.

"You know me already," he wheezed.

The only female in the band, Marla, keyboardist, couldn't be present at that time.

According to Mr Earl they didn't want to disturb the sanctity of Papparazzi's home more than this, so it would be most meaningful to continue the conversation taking a car ride together. The photographer contemplated for a moment whether he should throw the towel in at once. On the other hand, he wanted to call their bluff. He decided to seize the opportunity. Papparazzi put on his jacket and threw a side glance on his camera bag. Mr Earl saw it and nipped his intent in the bud. The photographer accepted his fate. The fact that he had his mobile phone in his pocket made his resolution easier. He could take pictures with it if needed. Outdoors he was directed to the back seat of a SUV beside Ramen and Pööpi. Mr Earl steered the vehicle and Lucas was in the codriver's seat. When the driver had changed his shoes to more appropriate ones for driving and put gloves on, the engine rolled on and the trip to the great unknown started off. When they reached Teboil in Ruskeasuo Mr Earl told that the whole existence of the group was based on disguising themselves just like, for instance, the Kiss. It was strictly forbidden to all of the members of The Earl to perform without their masks — from the very start.

"And then there you were with your camera in Tapiola. A wide range of thoughts ran through my mind when you swayed around me. It also crossed my mind that I could let Steel and Whip loose to charge you. They would have mangled you in that way that you would turn out to be a monster — an organic one."

The monster quadruplet cried out to laugh so loud that their masks jiggled. He felt intimidated. After they stopped the ringleader blurted out:

"No more games, okay! I never even thought about using such a violent means in order to get rid of you."

Afterwards Mr Earl had pulled all the strings to find out who was responsible and to stop the facial pictures publication. He had contacted *The Week* — all in vain.

"And then that son of a bitch magazine came out! I could not comprehend that Finland pulled this disgusting trick on our group! Our carefully built-up image was shattered to pieces. My world went so black that if you had been within reach of my long and creepy nails, I would have ripped you to shreds!"

Papparazzi tried to cut in the middle by stating the fact that the ice had been already broken in this matter in international publications.

"Who reads them in this country? Nobody! They are not taken in account!"

Mr Earl turned up his car radio.

"Our new music! It gets us in a better mood!"

The piece was Devil's Dark Light. The monsters were

moving to the music. The loud boom popped Papparazzi's ears, so he buried them under his hands. Lucas turned the volume down at last.

"We are eagerly looking forward to hear how the masses respond to this and other new material. *Killing Rainstorm* album will be coming out next year."

Mr Earl made a U-turn on the north side of Töölön Tulli. They returned back to where they had started. The following announcement was made.

"*The Week* makes a public apology in their next issue. They promise not to publish any private pictures of any of us. That keeps us satisfied. We are not going to take this thing further to the Judicial Chamber of Media or to sue them."

Papparazzi pressured on that nobody has committed a crime here. The band members were public figures in the deepest sense, including the one he had shot in a public place.

"You can always make a wish. The media can make a decision on their own discretion if they are taken into an account or not. In this case the action was reasonable, although they ignored your wishes. I am amazed that the magazine is now having second thoughts and begging your forgiveness."

"That's exactly what they are doing just now! And now we are clearing a ground to the reason why we are taking you on this ride."

"Well, why?"

"You are not on *The Week*'s payroll working on an entrepreneurial basis, that's why we want to make a wish to you that you'll take no more photos of us without our monster costumes."

Papparazzi chewed over the mafia style offer he practically wasn't able to refuse. The car was cramped and distressing. He was not ready to give an answer just yet; he wanted to bargain some time. He came up with the idea to go to have some advisory aid in Restaurant Tilkanranta. The suggestion gained support. The boombox went off so loud that the wax shot out of the ears.

The attention was guaranteed when they miraculously showed up in the bar and ordered drinks over the counter. Papparazzi cured his tinnitus with edible eardrops of Koskenkorva Viina. All the other members of the group made the same choice of shots. After timid initial confusion people started to gather around the black brotherhood. Autographs were distributed and photos were snapped. Papparazzi captured also the mixed entourage with his mobile phone camera. The joy was at its highest in the early hours when the whole place got excited singing one of the jingles of the thirsty heroes:

"We fed our faces with Kossu! We drank till morning! I guess you still remember it?"

None of them had a clear recollection how Papparazzi, Mr Earl, Lucas, Ramen and Pööpi worked their way into the flat of the first mentioned to crash in there. They had thrown their masks to the corner. Lucas and Pööpi sprawled on the couch, Ramen and Mr Earl snored on the soft-haired area rug beside them. Papparazzi slept fully clothed in his own bed in the bedroom.

The hangover worked as their alarm clock. Pööpi was the first to go to the loo taking a leak and throwing up. Some other living dead dragged themselves in there to drizzle. There were no other pukes. The bogey men came to the breakfast table one at a time snarling vaguely. Papparazzi was making an omelette with shaky hands and took coffee orders at the same time.

They cured their queasy condition with nips of booze.

Mr Earl retorted:

"You, Papparazzi, turned out to be a great fucking guy and socializer. As such that we allow you to take photos with our own faces."

The shooter couldn't believe what he was hearing.

"Oh, are you serious?"

"Yes, we are. When you were in the toilet we came to that conclusion. So, we are taking back that proposal we made to you in the car yesterday. Since we haven't had your answer so far there's no need to give it — ever!"

When the subjects had got ready, Papparazzi started buzzing around them at full speed. He took some of them on the balcony heading to the backyard. Lucas asked shyly:

"Uh... Now... To what magazine are you going to offer the pictures you took of us? As a professional you are considering it."

His answer was quick this time.

"Yes, I am. *The Week* came first in my mind but that might be the excluded option because they made their apology."

Mr Earl said decisively:

"It can be canmobile phoneed. I will contact the editorial office of the magazine today and announce to them that we regret all the fuss. If and when we get a good coverage from the next issue as ourselves, everybody wins."

Papparazzi shared their point of view.

"*The Week* will be more than pleased. The magazine will certainly give their consent on this swap."

Mr Earl promised to converge with Marla so her facial photo could be included as well.

"Marla has loads of them. You'll get them asap on email.

There will be no after talk if you claim them as your own."

"Always getting better! Thanks, pals!"

They celebrated this new found understanding with throwing high fives. Everything was okay in the Kingdom again.

THAI MASSAGE FROM HEAVEN

Best-selling author Joose Laaksonen lived a happy family life in southern France according to stories in magazines. Since he was more and more employed in TV programmes which meant that he was especially easy to spot in the capital while the programmes were recorded. Papparazzi had been able to capture the writer entering and exiting the Blue Lotus Massage — Thai massage salon in Fleminginkatu. Both times the beanstalk had looked nervously around — as if having a feeling that there might be somebody taking photos behind the bushes who could be on his heels. His hunch was right, but he hadn't been able to spot the Peeping Tom. He had been able to operate so inconspicuously sitting in his own car parked on the side of the street. After the wordsmith had vanished an idea flashed through Papparazzi's mind. A Thai massage could do a world of good to the shooter as well! At the same time, he could find out what kind of treatment Joose had got in the salon. That was something worth a lot of cash.

The scarf man stepped in and booked an appointment from a slim and beautiful Thai lady for the same massage as the previous customer. The lady led his client to a twilight room filled with the odour of joss sticks. Sounds of water rippling came out of the loudspeakers. Papparazzi peeled off his clothes and settled down on the massage table to be kneaded. He pointed out at his neck and back at its full length.

The lady attacked them with her oiled hands. Besides using her hands, she used her bodyweight. Since this was Papparazzi's first experience in this kind of milling he found that there was an endless amount of aching muscles and joints in his body. Tears welled in his eyes. The pain turned into pleasure at that point where he felt her strokes on his hips and thighs. Long coal black hair slid slenderly — tauntingly — along his lower back followed by a fierce dig on his buttocks.

The flowery beauty rolled Papparazzi over to his back. She went through his upper and lower body, one muscle group after another. When the paid time was due to be ending her fingers found their way first down on the root of his privates and then worked her way up. The massaged man whined with pleasure. The hand work ended with a happy ending. The screen of top secret had been dropped and the truth came out. A juicy story would arise from this! In Nice there would be an unhappy ending waiting: an angry wife waving a rolling pin.

THE BARGAIN COP TAKES A BLUNDER

Visibility on TV had made the Bargain Cop Viljo Säkkinen a household name. In *Redi* reality show he had been spotted to study the prices. Stinginess pulsed through his veins. He never hesitated to bend himself into a squatting position in order to dig the cheapest tuna fish tin from the lowest shelf.

Papparazzi was almost knocked over by surprise when he detected Viljo in the opening of The Mall of Tripla. He was wondering whether Viljo in his checked shirt, Stetson hat and leather jacket was going to switch sides? The observer decided to get to the bottom of it. He took the first pictures with his mobile phone camera while the skinflint signed autographs on the fan cards surrounded by his fans. When the buzz quieted down, he continued his way downstairs. The first place they entered was Prisma on the ground floor. The scrooge was in his own territory as much as he ever could be. He swept all the rates thoroughly. On the Service Market he filled his tummy with the free samples handed out freely. The delicatessen moment was captured on the camera. The customers twitched his sleeve and asked him news. He seemed to have all the time in the world to chitchat with them. Papparazzi pushed him nearer in order to hear what they were talking about. As it turned out Viljo visited Tripla with serious intentions. Some of the people were not delighted at his escapade. One of the old ladies gushed with her tits shaking:

"Oh, for God's sake! What on earth are you doing here? A Redi Man!"

It was made clear to the crowd that the production company might be interested in a change of scenery from the fishing port to Pasila. Viljo suspected that they had got a better offer from the newcomer. Personally, he was ready to skip town if needed. Money made him go around too.

"Is it cheaper here?"

"Not really. Today they do have more special offers, but I reckon the score will be even in the long run."

He said that he wasn't distracted by big percentage discount.

"After this kind of drop-downs you might end up to the normal rates. You should take a deal only when you get a quality product. Never buy rubbish."

It was time to get to the upper floors after chatting was finished. Papparazzi noticed on the stairs that the bargain hunter had got another shadow on his heels: a young security guard. The penny pincher might have been studying the price tags a little too carefully between the shelves, raising suspicion of a five-finger discount. On the Nordic Avenue the guard guided the archetype of stinginess aside. He wanted to take a peek into the fabric bag he was carrying. Papparazzi had a good spot for shooting. This was something worth talking about!

When Viljo returned from the side chambers to the crowd he lectured to the man in overalls.

"Didn't you really know who I am?"

He shook his head.

"I watch mostly Netflix."

The guard apologized many times over that he had taken the price hawk under his surveillance without a reason. He wasn't softened by his explanations.

"You can be certain that I will make a formal complaint! I won't recommend Tripla to the production company as being the new set of the TV show! I will continue to be a Redi man!"

There was a crowd gathering around the TV star. Most enthusiasts inquired what it was all about. There was a lot of bemoaning. Papparazzi was also listening near the hero. Viljo turned abruptly to the scarfed bloke:

"Did you get good photos of me?"

The surprise was whole-hearted but the tracker had no choice other than to nod.

"I tried to be as inconspicuous as I ever could. How did you spot me?"

"It takes one to know one!"

As it turned out photographing was also the scrooge's bread and butter. The celebrational and class photos were his priority. They decided to head off to exchange trade secrets over a cup of coffee. In Ciao! Caffe Papparazzi was also tipped how to get good bargains on his shopping.

At the opening and closing of sales you get the best discounts. Buying things outside the season is profitable: summer tyres in the winter and summer clothes in the fall. Remember always one thing in the shops: the more discount you get the less you pay.

THE GREAT FALL

Mimosa Kolu & Nerds whacked the first bars of the newest season of *The Fall* live TV show. The host Kake Vainio stepped into the spotlight accompanied by applause. The studio audience basked in the pictures waving signs of regards in their hands. The actors made an appearance and vanished to the backstage to change their costumes at hectic speed. In the first sketch ventured The Wonder Seven had on their colourful attire and wigs. The superheroes sang praises to mediocrity. It was time to cheer underachievers, the time of elitism was over. The *Hidden Lives* recording was shown just before the commercial break. The show went on with a vocal show of the actress Kaisa Lappalainen. She changed without delay her character from Chisu to Maija Vilkkumaa to Ellinoora and who knows who. Weekly News and the Serial Loser, the new section in the show, tickled the funny bones.

In the middle of everything the actors were caught off guard. They were commissioned to look for a familiar face from television, Perttu Lajunen. As Nikke Pyhälahti grabbed the disguised lurker something unexpected took place. Eggs started to fly towards Kake. One of them hit his forehead; the others flew past.

Papparazzi, who had been unnoticeably sitting on the stairs, ran to position and captured the dumbfounded host's face with the slimy gunk on his face. At lightning speed, he turned to zoom and to shoot how three young females stood up, popped their bare breasts and held up signs with a text: "How dare you, Kake?", "Shame on you, MTV3!" and "We demand justice!"

Exlamations waved among the audience. The protest and Egg Man 2.0 were something nobody could have anticipated. The studio host and a couple of members of the staff attacked the females. The slogans were twisted to hide them and the fiercely fighting protesters were removed from the auditorium. They sounded their battle cry:

"Me too!"

The staff shut them up, but once in a while one of them managed to get their voice heard. An extra commercial break was flapped on the commotion in Studio 135. Kake shook his head with astonishment. He and the stage were cleaned up in order to get them in cam condition. Papparazzi tried to follow the women and the staff escorting them out, but the stairs were packed with such a huge crowd that he wasn't able to push through. The police were reportedly on the scene and would take the troublemakers in their custody.

Me Too! group was formed by students of Gender Studies Stina Kontula, Lilli Arajuuri and Pipa Hentilä. The photographer dug up a text message he got from earlier that day: "Hi! Please do come to the set of live broadcasting of *The Fall* in Arabia industrial quarters tonight! We a going as a united female front against Kake Vainio and MTV3. The company made a really dumb decision to let Kake host *The Fall* after the fact that he is charged with a sex crime. This must be made right in a way nobody has ever seen before!"

Papparazzi's nose for news had started to tickle immediately. It hadn't betrayed him again this time judging from the fact that the tabloids begged him to give them pictures of the escapade as we speak. While the crowd returned to their seats he speeded up. He had to get somewhere quieter to answer the messages. He heard behind him that the programme continued with the Showcase portion of the show — and how distracted they were after the incident.

"And your hair!" Perttu the comedian cracked to Kake.

He couldn't connect anything on the impro that fitted like a glove. Especially since some loudmouth booed to the host. The mike man collapsed on the stage. A candy was stuck on a little starry-eyed viewer's throat. She pondered to her parents:

"Nobody was supposed to take a fall the first time on!"

THE BLUE AND WHITE MONA LISA

A French superstar and sex symbol Brigitte Bardot was known intimately as BB. Papparazzi was following closely somebody he called PS being the President's Spouse, the First Lady. He had spent quite a lot of his free time in order to capture crucial moments of PS's life — above all her enchanting and natural glow. It was more of a matter of feeling than reason.

He shot the presidential couple for the first time in The Big Apple Mall in Espoo. When Papparazzi spotted them there he rushed back to his car to get his camera gear in a jiffy.

In the checkout line they took the end place waiting their turn as everybody else. Somebody tried to give them their spot in the line but they graciously declined to take it. When their groceries emerged on the conveyer belt — milk, cheese, eggs, rye bread, sausage and magazines — Papparazzi pitched in. The security guards intervened and asked him to stop.

"Seeing the presidential couple doing shopping is such a rare sight that it simply screams to be captured," he argued.

Ultimately, he had no choice but to pack his gear into his bag.

His prompt action was rewarded. The photos sold well and some of them were published in newspapers.

Papparazzi did other gigs also taking pictures of the presidential couple. The blonde was not happy with his takings. Too much posing and stiffness. He could never stand out with those. He decided to focus on PS who was a mixture of beauty, style, power, unselfconsciousness and motherhood. The brunette melted people's hearts with her smile. The camera loved her. PS was Finland's Jackie!

Papparazzi took a guided garden tour to Kultaranta Castle in Naantali. It was the summer residence of the President. There was a flag flying on the tower which meant that the presidential couple was on the premises. He got barely nothing out of it.

He enjoyed a cup of coffee with pastry in idyllic Café Antonius. While circling his spoon in the coffee cup he understood how limited his options of shooting the First Lady were. In spite of that he decided to spend the rest of the day in the town centre. The market place and shop windows were scoured multiple times.

When having only an element of hope left Papparazzi spotted a black Mercedes pulling in front of R-Kioski in Tullikatu. The President stepped out and entered the shop. The cameraman intensified his steps and emerged on the side of the car in a jiffy. The amiable PS sat on the back seat. Papparazzi tapped her door. After a moment's hesitation the window opened. PS asked what he wanted. The shooter told her that he had come all the way from Helsinki to Naantali. Although there were thousands of roses in Kultaranta he hadn't been able to capture the most beautiful rose in the garden of them all i.e. PS. Could he remedy that defect here now?

PS gave a little laugh and promised him that he could take a couple of photos and then the window would be shut. The sun of Naantali was beating down for Papparazzi — as well from the sky as from the back seat. The driver followed closely the incident from the mirrors. Everything was all over when the head of state climbed back to the car. Blinker on and on the way. Papparazzi was delirious with happiness. A glimpse to the camera screen revealed that he had taken twenty frames instead of two. They would be published the next day for everybody to see.

The merits of pictures on Naantali's smile girl were acknowledged. Nobody else had taken photos equivalent to them. They also raised the question whether Papparazzi had crossed the line. Did he invade her privacy? The law of the land was to leave politicians' families in peace. The photographer zipped his mouth. The presidential couple did the same. The scribbling faded down quickly.

The golden rays of sun illuminated Mäntyniemi on a foggy morning. Papparazzi, dressed in camouflage, set his camera stand on the rock and took a long breath. It was good to be in nature. The president's residence's fenced area with gates and guardroom, a small parking area with road, a pond with water features and a kindergarten was visible in front of him. He used a long tube — as well as the day would be. He had taken beverages and a packed lunch with him.

Papparazzi made an effort to be as inconspicuous as he ever could. He was stalking his prey equal to an immobile predator and with sharp senses. He was hunting to get photos of the walking, jogging or cycling PS. The odds were against him; that was something he knew already. He had stood on guard many times before.

The main gate opened and the black official Mercedes emerged. The master of Mäntyniemi was in a hurry to attend to his important affairs. There was some other movement in the scenery. Presidential staff coming to work, children brought to kindergarten, also some random walkers and cyclists passed by in both directions. Soon the place was a haven of peace. The clock hands moved so slowly that Papparazzi had time to follow animal life, mostly squirrels and birds. Especially the humming of the winged flying creatures caught his attention. Sometimes they seemed to get agitated by something and fumbled away as one.

Then Midsummer and Christmas arrived simultaneously when PS emerged in her outdoor gear with Charlie the dog on a leash. The security personnel followed on the couple's heels. Papparazzi catapulted behind his camera. Fire! The pawed citizen strolled trustingly besides his mistress. Occasionally he stopped to sniff the ground. When the owner petted and scratched but also grabbed him in her arms, he was in the furry creature's heaven. The wind blew her hair cutely over her face. She was brimming over. Papparazzi captured all of this.

PS, the hairy personal trainer and the security person headed towards Seurasaari. The morning walk took about half an hour. Papparazzi got his best facial shots of the brunette when the trio returned to square one. He packed his stuff and took off from the scene. These takings would be the talk of the town!

PS's appearance in her new book of poems was blooming in the Academic Bookstore. There was a big crowd in the book house. There were quite a convenient number of media people present. The lyricist was wearing a stylish grey dress complemented with a red belt to give some colour. Papparazzi had prepared himself with care. He had read all mother of the country's previous collections which deepened his fan relationship even further. In the poems feelings and picturing nature were combined in a powerful way. The photographer sat at the end of the second row of seats. It gave him a good view of the lyricist.

PS told first that she was a very emotional writer. When a new poem was arising, it was a holistic feeling she could not evade and it had to be unbosomed on the paper. She had seen herself being linked on a chain of generations by poetry. Papparazzi worked intensely and tactfully. He used flashlight with consideration. The introduction of the book of poems culminated in carefully picked treats which rose to higher dimensions by her recitation. In the end the audience had a chance to ask questions from the author. One of the men wondered why there were no end rhymes in poetry anymore. First her heart missed a beat until she pulled herself together and explained that nobody had used them in decades. It wasn't forbidden to use them still. One of the young females stated directly her opinion of poetry. It was musty, fossil.

"Why don't you turn to rap? You could reach the young readers more easily."

The author was going to stay with the traditional style.

"I don't own the rap as a natural form of expression for myself. But you are right in the fact that you can hear relaxed rhyming mainly in it. There is no reason why poetry couldn't let go on a similar way."

The book audience burst into applause.

A granny with round specs asked how the presidential spouse took the sensational photos.

"You are a weekly sight in yellow press. This was not so before. What has happened to you?"

PS's facial expression stiffened and blushed. She pointed her finger at Papparazzi.

"It's all his fault!"

All the glances turned towards the photographer who was ambushed red handed.

"What have you to say to that accusation, young man?" the granny questioned.

Papparazzi rolled on his chair uncomfortably. In his opinion this kind of grilling was against the spirit of the occasion. He pressured that he was here on a photographing job. He aimed to revolve the attention he got to somewhere else.

"The hero stands in there, in the forefront."

Nothing helped. Since PS declared that she had no wish to be a photobomber.

"But there is nothing I can do if a paparazzo follows me around."

"It is Papparazzi!"

Tensions mounted. The pulps were told to have gone too far. The high-end politician's family members should be left in peace. They demanded Papparazzi a good explanation for his actions. The pressure in the kettle rose until the cover opened a little.

"Hands up if you haven't seen my pictures of Emma?"

Not one was raised. The ripple of conversation faded away.

"This is enough, thank you!"

Papparazzi's literary party was over. He didn't stay in the line to wait for an autographed brand new book.

The towhead photographer sat on guard on a wooden bench across the Supreme Court building. The Finnish flag was wagging on the top of the President's Castle. There were also two soldiers standing in front of the castle in their parade uniforms. These both indicated that the President was in the building. Otherwise Papparazzi wouldn't have been present. He had circled the castle quarter several times. You could never know if The First Lady miraculously showed up in Northern Esplanade, Helenankatu, Aleksanterinkatu or Mariankatu. Papparazzi had no idea whether the brunette was in the castle at all.

Tick tock. Fatigue made his eyelids droop. On the verge of sleep, he realized he was catching a glimpse of something extremely significant. His gaze was invigorated. The First Lady walked along Northern Esplanade. Papparazzi rushed after her. He followed her at a suitable distance in order to make sure that she wouldn't take a glimpse of him even by mistake. He contemplated feverishly the right approach on the matter. If he burst right in front of her taking a picture she would put on her sunglasses and the game would be over. As it were the eyes were the mirror of the soul.

He hailed a taxi and told the driver to keep on the side of the brunette. The window open and the tube sticking out of the window pointing at the stepper. His camera played in major. He got pictures of the First Lady's side profile — it was clear that she couldn't hear the clicking of the shutter release in the middle of traffic noise. Near Mannerheimintie the driver hit the brakes and honked. Papparazzi was so focused on his own doing that he couldn't tell whether it was for the will to put her eyes on him or it was somebody acting like a jerk in the traffic. The brunette gazed upon the taxi as the shooter was up to speed. Top shots were bound to came. The secretly filmed lady noticed Papparazzi that exact second, turned her head away and hid her beautiful eyes behind sunglasses. The moment was over.

The cab took the camera guy back to the hoods of the

castle. He was so exhilarated that he tipped the driver generously.

Papparazzi studied the day's harvest. There was one photo above the rest. PS appeared in that one from top to toe. She walked forward looking over her shoulder straight to the camera. Right hand bent from the elbow holding her sunglasses. On her face there was light field makeup; a smile played quietly on her lips and radiantly in her eyes. The wind played with her hair on her left cheek and chin. She was wearing a jet-black shirt, light jeans and blue sneakers with white laces. Emma strode on the spot of an empty parking space, behind which was a display window of a clothing store. The general impression was enchanting.

Papparazzi named the vertical picture The Blue And White Mona Lisa. He pressed its print against his chest, burning with excitement. It would be the most sold, published, acknowledged and spoken of his photos. The perfect Papparazzi moment!

Wine glasses were raised for the congratulating clinks in Gallery Papparazzi. The Blue And White Mona Lisa exhibition was officially open. The house was full, and on the floor swelled a sea of flowers. The presidential couple honoured the occasion with their presence. Emma was wearing a blue and white dress and the president a blue toned suit with a discreet checked pattern. They both looked radiant and happy. Photographers and reporters surrounded them on the spot of movable partition. On it was hanging the picture that gave the name to the exhibition. The father and the mother of the country posed beside it. The flashes blinked constantly.

Papparazzi and Mandi had received the guests at the door. Since there had been edgier moments during the shooting of the exhibited photos the first mentioned had anticipated hearing some words of retribution from the ruler or his spouse. Their small talk was just casual. The President referred to an earlier confidential message that indicated that the office he was leader of would acquire The Blue And White Mona Lisa no matter the cost. On the top of the highest bid he could always put ten thousand euros. On his words of welcome the photographer quoted Ralph Waldo Emerson:

"Loving beauty shows taste. Creating beauty is art."

The guests strolled freely looking around the creations and having a chitchat. They sipped their wine slowly. The works were commented on and favourites chosen. Others than the opus magnum got support. The state of Papparazzi was perplexed and surrealistic. At the same time, he was proud of his artwork hanging on the walls. The exhibitions and life of an artist brought great variety to his core work.

A couple of months after the opening Papparazzi received a festive letter from the President of the Republic and his missus. The camera hero was invited to The Independence Day Banquet in President's Castle. The tribute was so overwhelming that he keeled over on the spot.

IT WASN'T ME — IT WAS THE PEN!

"If you are tired of London, you are tired of life."

This, Samuel Johnson's statement from the 18th century, was still valid. Papparazzi took photos of the statue of the author behind the St Clement Danes Church. These would go to his home album. The scarfed bloke asked a young girl passing by to capture photos of him and Johnson. Papparazzi picked his notebook in his left hand holding it with all of his five fingers. His right hand he clenched into a fist as British Icon. The photos together were photogenic.

Papparazzi was on holy ground, Fleet Street. For a long time, it had been the most predominant media street. They had published newspapers there for over 300 years. The last of the reporter Mohicans had left a few years back. He could see with the eyes of his soul capped newsies selling the papers and reporters running with sore feet after scoops. Pens, notepads, cameras, telegrams, telephones and so forth passed as a filmstrip before his eyes.

In their memoirs the journalists pictured their work in Fleet Street being an adventure. They had given it their brains and hearts — everything. Some of them lost their families, their health, their lives. The gossip and news travelled from other parts of England and the world fast. If you got your foot in the door of editorial and slipped in, you would not leave at no cost. It had been beneficial for all of the newspaper houses to operate at close proximity to each other. If nothing else it had been useful to see how the neighbours rushed with burning rubber to a place of news. They had followed and got a head start on the buddy next to you.

Papparazzi woke up to the present moment. His gaze didn't meet anyone with a resemblance of a journalist. The digitalized media had no need for closeness. The action was effective anyway. Fleet Street was as lively as always. There were so many passers-by that it was difficult to squeeze oneself in. The tourist buses honked. Papparazzi was searching signs that the press had left behind in the midst of the crowd. The Fleet Street Press Café made his heart beat faster. The name was fitting since it honoured the printing ink smelling past. There were clock dials everywhere along the way. Time was essential to a journalist; the news was in a hurry, Papparrazzi contemplated while glancing at them briefly. Some of them were showing the wrong time. Was it an act of floppiness or deliberate? An urge to send a message that times had changed? The questions were floating in the air infinitely.

Papparazzi lifted and lowered his camera at a brisk pace while walking. He captured hundreds of photos.

On a wall of red brick bulding stood names of the newspapers: *Sunday Post*, *People's Friend*, *People's Journal* and *Dundee Courier*. The press people had named the oldest Irish pub in London The Tipperary after The First World War. The song It's a Long Way to Tipperary, which the pub's name referred to, started to hum in Papparazzi's ears as an earworm. The song's lyrics told about an Irish man who came to London. In the joyful beat of the city his longing to go back to his sweetheart — the most beautiful girl of all — on the green island scorched his breast. The letters travelled across the Irish Sea and the man, head over heels in love, reminded her in one of the letters that if there was something wrong in his sentences it wasn't the writer's fault. It wasn't me, it was the pen!

The house of the *Daily Express* bathed in sunlight. Although there were no news authors employed in the building, its showy appearance gleamed as a beacon of the freedom of speech to Papparazzi. He had taken peeks on the side alleys and streets while walking on the street, rarely straying on them. There was still one place he could not pass, St Bride's Church dedicated to journalists. From a wooden bench in the chapel he admired the altar and the skilful glass painting above it. The saints and cherubs sculptured around. Gold glimmered everywhere. A memorial nook honouring those journalists who had lost their lives pulled his mind low. There were casualties also from recent years. A quotation from the Bible touched deep: "The Word became flesh and lived among us."

The Old Bell pub offered an amusing contrast to the previous place. A ripple of conversation met him right at the door. Jugs were knocked together in hearty fashion. The furnishing of the lively old pub was dark and earthy. Papparazzi sat by the window to enjoy a chicken dish accompanied with pale lager. He had enjoyed the traditional pub dishes so often that he needed a change. An elegant elderly gentleman was attacking his dessert beside him. An apple pie with whipped cream wasted away very slowly. Every mouthful brought a party in the mouth. After hesitation and disposition, they introduced themselves. The gentleman was Neil Scott, a retired employee in Fleet Street.

"I had a full life in *Sunday Post*. I came here to relive fond memories."

"Well, that's funny! I am your photographing colleague from Finland. I have the greatest respect for Fleet Street; that is why I am making a pilgrimage here."

As it turned out the retiree had always been a bit of a dandy.

"They called me Wannabe Hercule Poirot. With the dark hair we resemble each other quite a lot, but unlike the famous detective I never let my moustache grow."

He never showed up to work without a white shirt and a necktie. As well as that he had always found a pen from his breast pocket.

Due to never knowing when you needed it. Usually when you least expected it.

Papparazzi nodded as a mark of acceptance. He certainly knew what it was like to expect the unforeseen.

From early on Neil had been nicknamed as the news cannon.

"I was irreverent in my work so that no piece of important news ever slipped past my eyes. The news is the core of the paper. When you forget it, you are at the beginning of the end."

On his career he had seen the golden years of the press world and lived to see the change.

"Wiping your screen is this day. It is hard for me to accept it that there are fewer and fewer people who rustle paper in their hands."

A moment's silence settled down at the round wooden table.

"A truly and genuinely independent press is a very exotic flower to be tended with care and love. In the wrong hands it is easy to let it wither or kill it."

Although they were citizens of different countries congeniality brought them together. The pen and the camera were weapons of defending the truth and true for both of them. In a tight spot they would use them even at the expense of their lives. They both agreed that there would be no modern press without Fleet Street.

When the Brit had cleaned his saucer, he thanked the Finn for having somebody to talk to, stepped up from the table and patted his chest.

"Still carrying the pen. You never know what will happen next on Fleet Street."

They both chuckled. The door slammed shut after Mr Scott, and Papparazzi focused on his lunch grown cold.

The last leg on his pilgrimage was Ludgate Circus where Fleet Street and three other streets met. The old decorative buildings and contemporary office buildings coexisted peacefully surrounding the crossing. Business atmosphere flourished. Papparazzi headed right from the red phone box towards the Blackfriars underground station. In front of him was a mounted policeman in a yellow vest. The hooved constable had nerves of steel. That was something required from Papparazzi when he returned to his daily job the same day. *The Week* had texted him that a former sports caster and a current sports nut Kuisma Rytölä had escaped in Adam's dress from the nude beach of Seurasaari. The last sighting of him had been near Papparazzi's hoods. Since the cameraman knew the area through and through they wanted to know if that kind of gig suits him. An OK acknowledgement roared off.

www.ingramcontent.com/pod-product-compliance
Lightning Source LLC
LaVergne TN
LVHW091548060526
838200LV00036B/747